# Curse of the Moon

## by

## Beth Trissel

*The Secret Warrior Series*

**Curse of the Moon**

Contact Information: info@thewildrosepress.com

Cover Art by *Debbie Taylor*

The Wild Rose Press, Inc.
PO Box 708
Adams Basin, NY 14410-0708
Visit us at www.thewildrosepress.com

Publishing History
First Climbing Rose Edition, 2016
Print ISBN 978-1-5092-0759-6
Digital ISBN 978-1-5092-0760-2

*The Secret Warrior Series*
Published in the United States of America

**"Maybe you're an *Allasomorph*,"**
Jimmy suggested. "They have their own planet and several moons."

"Great. Because I'm not weird enough?"

A scraping noise and the kitchen door opened, letting in the autumn chill and Jackson's highly unusual grandmother. Miriam held a basket of eggs gathered from the red and bronze chickens in the sturdy coop out back. Her slender figure was wrapped in a gray wool shawl, her lined face rosy beneath the matching scarf knotted at her throat. Her long silver hair and blue, beaded skirts whipped in the wind.

She shut the heavy door and glanced at the assembly around the table. Brown eyes, the dark hue of Jackson's, rested on Morgan. Her gaze widened, then narrowed in an expression of somber awareness. "Oh my."

If anyone apart from the unfathomable Chief Okema possessed the knowledge to aid her, it was this gentle healer. Wisdom flowed through Miriam's veins like clear mountain water. Not only was she Jackson's grandmother, but a descendent of the Star People, a mysterious race of space aliens Okema prophesied would someday return. What that meant for Miriam, and ultimately Jackson, Morgan didn't know. Only that without help from this wise woman, or someone, she was doomed to a whole other world of weird.

## Praise for Beth Trissel

"This is a series with a whole bunch of potential and I can't wait to read more. Definitely recommended for all fans of YA/Paranormal."

*~Merissa, YA Insider*

~*~

"If you like Native American stories, shape shifters, curses, living in the mountains and woods, a little violence, semi immortality, action and adventure then this might be for you!"

*~Kelly, Kindle & Me*

~*~

"A quick, fun read with a swoon-worthy romantic interest and some kickass moments and shapeshifters!"

*~Dani Reviews Things (for THE HUNTER'S MOON)*

## Dedication

To my dear daughter, Elise,
whose support was a great help
in the writing of this story.

## Acknowledgements

A special thank you to Jim Great Elk Waters, Shawnee Elder and Pipecarrier, for his valuable assistance with the Shawnee language used in this book.

Chapter One
Wandering Wolf

*Late October, Wapicoli Lodge, Virginia Mountains*

"Sensors indicate Morgan may be an anthromorph." From across the breakfast table in the colonial era kitchen, ten-year-old Jimmy imitated the noise made by a *Star Trek* tricorder.

Morgan glanced from her partially demolished plateful of bacon and eggs to her sci-fi/comic book obsessed brother. "What gave me away, Batboy?"

His blue eyes surveyed her through black rimmed glasses beneath tousled blond hair. "Hint, hint. 'Oh, Grandmother, what big ears you have.'"

"Drat. Not again." Likening herself to *Little Red Riding Hood* went *poof* last week after learning she was, in fact, the doggone wolf.

She laid down her fork and patted either side of her head. Sure enough, her ears were furry and pointed upward.

"Crapola. How could I not even notice?" She was slipping in and out of wolfdom with less thought than it took to pull on a pair of gloves.

She sought Jackson's currently totally unwolfish face on the other side of the handcrafted table. Firelight from the brick hearth dappled the long black hair he wore loose around his broad shoulders over a rugged plaid shirt. His Native American good looks seemed to heighten every time she was near him. How must she appear in comparison, sitting here with wolf ears?

A groan escaped her. "What am I gonna do?"

Sympathy crinkled his dark eyes. "We'll think of something. Don't worry."

"Wish I shared your confidence." She dropped her hand and grasped her fork. "I'm not totally freaked out yet, but getting there. Fast."

"You'll be all right." His encouraging smile showed his dimples and enhanced his appeal.

"But I can't seem to remain fully human."

He took a sip of fragrant coffee from the blue pottery mug. "Technically, you're not."

"I mean, appear human when I wish. Like you."

His cousin, Hawthorne, leaned toward her, one elbow on the table, his greenish gray eyes alight. "Probably just a phase."

"What am I? Five? I'm a little old for phases."

"At least it's not your nose." Hawthorne seldom took anything seriously.

"It was last night." Kind of a shock when she'd glimpsed her reflection in the mirror.

He chuckled. "Oh, man. I'd like to have seen that."

Annoyance flashed through her. "Really? You probably will soon enough. Up. Close. And personal," she bit out. "Fangs too, if you're extra lucky."

That dimmed the sparkle in his far too cheery expression.

"No need to go all neon blue on me, Morgan," he chided, referring to her glow-in-the dark eyes when she was *wolfing out*. "I was only kidding around."

"LOL," she muttered.

Skimming past her, Jimmy returned his attention to Hawthorne. "So, anyway. Which do you wanna be, *the Joker* or *the Penguin*?" he persisted, forging ahead in their previous discussion.

"Dude, enough with the super villain debate," Hawthorne shushed him. "Morgan's seriously wigging here. And I've got dibs on *Wolverine*," he couldn't resist adding.

Jimmy high-fived his partner in geekhood. "Roger that. I've been leaning more toward *Iron Man* lately."

"For what? Halloween?" she tossed back.

They both eyed her as if she'd missed the obvious. "What else? *Comic Con's* not until July." The whiz kid would know.

She rolled her eyes. "Like either of you have the money to go."

"Thus the big party we're gearing up for at the lodge." Jimmy appeared slightly wounded.

"Perfectly suitable for you, Jimbo," Jackson assured him, with a hand on his pint-sized shoulder. "Not sure Hawthorne can handle all the excitement, though. Past his bedtime."

"I'll manage." Hawthorne shook his long hair, a shade lighter than Jackson's, and crossed both arms over his chest. "Tick tock, mighty leader. We're still waiting for you to pick who you wanna be."

Jimmy bounced expectantly on his perch between the two guys, the closest he had to brothers. "How about *Batman*? Or hey—Robin Hood? You're the best archer, Jackson."

"I am not wearing green tights," he said flatly.

*Even Jackson was distracted by the big eve!*

Morgan threw her arms up, her right hand now a

3

white paw. "For crying out freaking loud! Jimmy will be clanking around in tin cans. Lord only knows how Hawthorne will make himself up as *Wolverine*, and Jackson can pull off whatever look he wants. Meanwhile, I could use some help here."

Three heads swiveled in her direction. "Whoa. Definitely phenomenal." Jimmy's freckled face scrunched in concentration. "I'll take more readings. See what I can come up with."

"Thanks." She clasped the paw in her still-human hand. "Your brilliant mind might contrive something. So far, the only way I've found to regain 'normal' is to concentrate on an image of myself as I usually appear."

"Mind over matter. Cool." Jimmy exuded enthusiasm.

"Yeah. But it's draining. Takes a lot of brainpower."

"Maybe with practice, you can do it in a nanosecond. Even bend spoons," he suggested.

She frowned at him. "This is not *The Matrix*. At least, I don't think it is. Let me focus."

Jackson motioned for silence. "Go ahead."

Her onlookers waited in anticipation.

Squeezing her eyes shut, she pictured the girl she remembered before the change, blonde hair, blue eyes, no fur, and fully recognizable human features. She pushed back 'the ice queen', as she'd dubbed her inner wolf, refusing a glimpse of the creature in her mind's eye. That prima donna was likely responsible for this whole darn mess.

"What about now?" She blinked, and glanced around.

The trio shook their heads.

Hawthorne's lips twitched. "The ears are still there. But kudos on getting your hand back."

Hope plummeted. "For how long? Dang it."

Jackson reached across the table and captured her fingers in his reassuring grasp. "We'll find a way through this."

"We'd better, and soon." This wasn't at all what she'd anticipated when dreading 'the change'. The thrill she'd experienced bounding to the top of the ridge with him and the rest of the pack during the full moon was fading as this new insane reality set in.

Lifting his arm, he smoothed her furry ears. His every touch sent tiny shivers through her, but the last thing she felt at this moment was sexy. "Come on, Morgan. They're not so bad," he coaxed, in his low country drawl. "Kind of cute."

"Seriously, Jackson?"

He crossed his heart, the way he did whenever she used that expression. "Don't worry about the Wapicoli. The clan will cut you some slack. You're a newbie. I've been at this since I was sixteen. Heading to eighteen in January."

"Ding! Ding! Birthday alert," Hawthorne chimed.

Morgan rounded on him. "Why aren't you sprouting wolf ears? You haven't been sixteen all that long. And it's not as if you're incredibly mature for your age."

Kindling in the fireplace hissed and popped as he shrugged. "Guess I'm mature enough, Wolf Girl."

She preferred it when Jackson used the name he'd given her, although the Shawnee version was unpronounceable.

He chewed his cornbread with a pensive air,

chasing the swallow with a sip of coffee. "It's not only from when we turn sixteen that counts. We also have added prep time to consider."

"Like practically since we were born," Hawthorne added.

She stabbed the fork at her bacon. "Being a *loup-garou* is easy peasy for you and Jackson in comparison to me."

A grin split Jimmy's face. "Mademoiselle Devereux—Morgan's sophomore French teacher—would be impressed."

"That I recall the term or that I'm a werewolf?"

"Both," he answered between bites. "But mostly your pronunciation. The French are all about accent."

"Even they might notice my turning into a primal predator." She returned to her breakfast with scant interest in the food, only knowledge that her hunger must be satisfied.

Another thing to get used to, eating like a wolf. And scents were one hundred times their former potency. Fragrances vied with each other in the kitchen, from meaty aromas to the braided onions and bunches of dried herbs hanging from the blackened beams overhead.

Each of her three companions had their own scent. Jackson's masculine essence was deeply stirring. Jimmy's familiar aroma meant family, and Hawthorne's spoke of friendship, when he wasn't annoying the mess out of her.

She bent back toward Jackson. "So, neither of you have ever had to deal with what I am, even a little?"

He shook his head. "The *no unauthorized attack on human's thing* is enough."

"How about any other newly turned werewolf?" She'd settle for one kindred spirit.

His brow creased and his lips pursed pityingly. "None I know of. Sorry."

*Hang it all*! She didn't want pity, just the closest thing to normalcy a werewolf could expect. "Holy moly. I'm on my own freakin' planet."

"Maybe you're an *Allasomorph*," Jimmy suggested. "They have their own planet and several moons."

"Great. Because I'm not weird enough?"

A scraping noise and the kitchen door opened, letting in the autumn chill and Jackson's highly unusual grandmother. Miriam held a basket of eggs gathered from the red and bronze chickens in the sturdy coop out back. Her slender figure was wrapped in a gray wool shawl, her lined face rosy beneath the matching scarf knotted at her throat. Her long silver hair and blue, beaded skirts whipped in the wind.

She shut the heavy door and glanced at the assembly around the table. Brown eyes, the dark hue of Jackson's, rested on Morgan. Her gaze widened, then narrowed in an expression of somber awareness. "Oh my."

If anyone apart from the unfathomable Chief Okema possessed the knowledge to aid her, it was this gentle healer. Wisdom flowed through Miriam's veins like clear mountain water. Not only was she Jackson's grandmother, but a descendent of the Star People, a mysterious race of space aliens Okema prophesied would someday return. What that meant for Miriam, and ultimately Jackson, Morgan didn't know. Only that without help from this wise woman, or someone, she was doomed to a whole other world of weird.

Zeroing in on Morgan, she set the basket on the sideboard laden with dishes of cornbread, bacon, and scrambled eggs. "How long has this been going on?"

"For several days," Morgan confessed, "but it's worsening."

"Yes. It would."

The gravity in the older woman's manner intensified the apprehension mounting in Morgan. "Why?"

"You have something few have ever heard of called *Wandering Wolf*. In Shawnee, it's *Pab'amose M'wewa*. In Latin, *Vagantem Lupus*."

Morgan could hardly believe what Miriam was saying. "Sounds like a disease."

"Not an illness, a condition. A potentially serious one, known from ancient times."

Sobering realization sank in. "Explains the Latin."

Miriam nodded. "The condition dates back to early Rome. Founded, according to legend, by twin boys left to die who were rescued by a she-wolf."

"Right. Romulus and Remus." This much Morgan recalled from school. An unsettling thought occurred; that wolf might have been human, once.

Heaviness weighted her chest, and a hush fell over the others, now intently focused on her. "There must be a way out of this predicament."

She lifted the moonstone at her throat, suspended by the delicate silver chain. Glints of heavenly light shone from the blue gem. The phenomenal gift came to her by way of Sarah Morgan, her great grandmother six times removed. Exactly how the stone ended up with Sarah, Morgan couldn't explain. She'd been near death at the time. The whole episode was like a dream now.

"Can this help me?" Maybe Miriam knew how to tap into the stone's mystical power to aid her.

The older woman shook her head. "The moonstone's greatest use lies in strengthening life, not reducing the wolf."

All three guys shifted their solemn gaze between Morgan and Miriam. Jackson spoke first. "What does this mean for Morgan, Grandma?"

"She will worsen, unless we halt the progression of her condition. Precious time is lost," she reproached Morgan. "You should have told me sooner."

"I'm sorry. I thought I could handle this myself." An assumption she regretted more every moment.

Jackson waved aside her apology. "It's also my fault. I should have spoken up the instant I realized. The question is, where to go from here. Is there an herbal cure you know of?"

"One." Miriam draped her scarf beside the egg basket. "A tincture of wolfsbane and mistletoe."

His eyebrows rose, then drew together. "Aren't those plants deadly poisons?"

"In too great a dose. A werewolf can tolerate only a miniscule amount, less than a human. But a potion from these herbs will hinder the wolf, until Morgan gains more control."

His dusky complexion paled. "Can you administer the proper dose?"

"I believe so." The furrows in Miriam's brow deepened, and she hesitated. "Only, I'm no longer in possession of the tincture. And we have scant time for me to obtain these rare herbs and brew a new elixir in the correct proportions."

He ran a hand through his hair. "Does anyone have it?"

"Lilith Dubois."

Jaws dropped in the collective circle, and everyone gaped at Miriam.

"Good heavens," Morgan breathed out, her heart palpating as if she had an arrhythmia. "The Lizard Lady."

"Also known as the *Mountain Witch*. And make no mistake, she is one evil witch. *Matchee'midewininì*." The Shawnee term combined with Miriam's expression was doubly forbidding.

Jackson squared his shoulders. "Even so, if Lilith's the only person with the cure, then we must go to her."

"Yes." Morgan squeezed the assent from her tight throat.

"Remember, Lilith will not give you what you seek for nothing," Miriam cautioned. "She'll want something in return."

"Greedy b—" Jackson broke off. "What have we got that's tempting enough?"

A cherished legacy came to mind. She smoothed the moonstone at her throat. "This?"

"Never!" Miriam's emphatic refusal startled her. The usually mild woman thrust a finger at her. "You cannot allow Lilith to have that sacred stone at any cost. It's a gift from the Star People to will as they see fit, and they have chosen you. We do not yet know all its power. Until Sarah Morgan channeled the stone to you, the night of your change, we thought it lost."

"What then?" Morgan was almost afraid to ask.

The righteous wrath radiating from Miriam lessened slightly. "That remains to be seen, but guard the stone. Always. I fear this trip to Lilith bodes no good. Above all things, she desires power. Okema has kept her at bay, but his strength lessens. He's late in his seventh lifetime. It is up to you and Jackson." She swept a hand at the foursome. "To all of you, to secure the Wapicoli clan from the Mountain Witch."

Jackson pressed the tips of his fingers against his forehead. "While getting what we need from her. And defeat the murderous Panteras, enemy werewolves, and whatever or whoever else threatens us. No biggie."

"Not all must be accomplished in a day," his grandmother amended. "Much is asked of you, yet much is given. Remember this."

His chest rose and fell. "I know."

"Do you truly?" Miriam laid a hand on his head, as if in blessing. "Never forget, you are the seventh in our line, the most powerful Wapicoli, destined to assume Okema's place, in time." She gestured at Morgan. "And you are the seventh Morcant. You have no idea what you are capable of. The wolf within you is strong, the reason you suffer from *Pab'amose M'wewa.*"

"I think I preferred the Latin term."

"Call it what you will, *Wandering Wolf* must be overcome. You and the ice queen, as you call her, must work together as one, or she will completely take you over."

Morgan swallowed hard. "And I will cease to be?"

"I fear so. Harness her power. Do not succumb to it. For this, you need help." Miriam was unbending.

Chills scattered down Morgan's spine. "Then we have a trip to make to The Lizard Lady. What else can we do?"

No one offered any other suggestions.

Despite the grim state of affairs, Morgan noted Hawthorne didn't fully suppress a smile. She recalled his proclaimed affection for Lilith's youngest daughter, Dilly, and Jackson's stern chastisement. Lilith also had a second daughter, Eve. Were the girls as bad as their mother, or better?

Jackson turned his dark gaze on Morgan. "You'll be OK. We'll get what we need."

The hard set of his mouth wasn't promising. Did he really believe she'd be all right? And what if she weren't?

Alarm beat in Morgan like the pounding of a Shawnee drum.

Chapter Two
The Barter

What was keeping the guys? Tired of pacing the lodge like, well, a caged wolf, waiting for them to appear, Morgan rapped on their bedroom door.

"'Speak friend and enter,'" Jimmy replied, quoting Gandalf in *The Lord of the Rings*.

"Friend! Soon to be foe, if you all don't get a move on." She swept into the room. "We're burning daylight, boys."

That wasn't all they were burning, including incense, judging by the odors assailing her. The woodsy spice of cedar, the soothing lumber heavily used in her bedroom, blended with the pungent aromas typical of teenage males. Castoff socks, shorts, and t-shirts could use a soak in hot soapy water with whatever you bathed a skunk-sprayed dog in. High-powered deodorant lingered in the air. The guys weren't into herbs for that amenity. Candles lent light and gave off a welcome piney fragrance, along with the cone of incense trailing thin smoke.

Were they conducting some sort of pre-visit to the Lizard Lady ritual?

The trio had supposedly assembled in here to access their inventory for the afternoon outing. The benefit of the potentially dangerous encounter with this she-devil outweighed the risk if Lilith held the key to a cure for *Wandering Wolf.* Morgan understood precautions must be taken before they left, but for how long? Every moment cost her.

In the assault of scents, one drew her like a pheromone. Jackson's unique musk was darn near irresistible, but the date night she'd dreamed of would have to wait. Again.

She ran a critical eye over the weapons piled in the center of the room. Essential, but she expected their innate skills, plus Jimmy's wits, were their best defense—or a magic wand, which they lacked. Batboy didn't strike her as particularly industrious, perched on a stool made of stout twigs in front of a plank top desk playing a video game on the computer. Lights flashed from the screen as he worked the mouse.

*There.* Beside him were the protective sunglasses meant for her. He'd improvised them with mirrors fitted onto flip down visors to guard against the hypnotic gaze of the gorgon like witch. This way, Morgan could view Lilith's reflection and monitor her movements without falling prey to her mind control. A twist on the old 'turn people to stone' thing, yet equally hazardous. One disadvantage to the glasses, she'd have to stand backward to see forward. Still, it was a brilliant innovation.

As for the others, Jackson had said he and Hawthorne—all the Wapicoli, in fact—slid furtive glances at Lilith from the corners of their eyes, like Border collies herding sheep. They followed her every step, each gesture, bur never face-to-face. Tricky to master, and an imperfect system, but 'needs must', as Miriam said. Until Morgan learned to avoid direct eye contact, she had the glasses. Jimmy intended to don his night vision goggles to screen out the harmful gorgon rays.

Hawthorne sat cross-legged on the hardwood floor, thumbing through the comics stacked against the log wall beside Jimmy's rumpled cot. He'd been appointed to help batboy create the special glasses. Clearly, they were done.

So, what was the holdup?

She scanned the rustic room. The electronics made a striking contrast to the log walls and furnishings handcrafted by the Wapicoli. An unlikely meld of old and new.

*Ah*, the hitch lay with Jackson. Fingers threaded behind his head, he was prone on the bottom bunk of the double-decker log bed he shared with Hawthorne. He stretched the length of the mattress on the handwoven red wool blanket with black silhouettes of animals embellishing the design. The stare he projected at the bunk overhead meant something troubled him.

Worse than worry over her? He hadn't even glanced around at her arrival.

Smothering an impatient groan, she sank onto the buckskin beanbag chair beside the arsenal of bows, arrows, tomahawks, and sheathed knives heaped on the floor. The sweeping tail she'd acquired, and couldn't rid herself of, made sitting in a chair awkward. Worse, wearing her leather pants was impossible.

She'd been forced to step into the long blue skirt and thick flannel petticoat Miriam dug up for her from an antique leather trunk. Morgan had roped both garments in at the waist with ties. How many yards of wool went into the skirt and the hooded green cloak around her shoulders, she couldn't imagine. A lot of sheep had been sheared.

'Might as well have the whole outfit,' Miriam had concluded, throwing in the long-sleeved, white linen shift Morgan wore beneath the brown-striped bodice laced up her front. The shift hung to her knees under the petticoat and skirt, and doubled as a blouse. The vintage getup must've belonged to a woman from the eighteenth century.

Heck, Morgan would fit right in with reenactors, except for the tail trying to protrude through her skirt. Not many colonials were werewolves. The canine-like ears were also a giveaway, but concealed under the ruffled white cap Miriam had added for that extra special touch. Any level of *cool* Morgan had ever achieved—however briefly—was gone. Nada, zip, zilch. *Bon voyage*. That ship had sailed.

Jimmy neglected his game long enough to give her the once over from behind his black glasses. "Good grief, Morgan. Should we have Scotty beam you up?"

She grimaced. "I vote for beaming me aboard if we—" She waved at the assembly. "Don't get a move on."

"I know, I know. We need to go." Jackson was fixated on the top bunk as if the mattress held what he sought.

"That's for shooting sure," Jimmy said over his shoulder, once again immersed in zapping zombies, or whatever they were.

A muttering groan sounded from Jackson.

Hawthorne set his comic aside. "Did I detect an aarrgghh in that?"

"You'd detect far worse if I wasn't watching my mouth," Jackson snapped.

"Bad words, bad words," Hawthorne supplied.

Jackson threw his hands up. "I've combed the lodge for treasure, and racked my brains. Still can't think what to trade in exchange for the potion. You can't show up at Lilith's empty-handed. We've got to have something to barter."

"Gold is a currency that never loses its value." Jimmy sounded like an infomercial. "I say we give her doubloons."

Hawthorne reached for another comic. "We'd have to rob the Mountain Panteras—the ones with the leftover pirate booty. Which means we'd have to storm their rocky fortress."

"We don't have time to storm anything. Particularly not the stronghold of panther shifters." Morgan glanced out the window at the watery sun sinking lower above the tree line. "If we wait much longer, it'll be dark and I'll sprout something else. Doesn't the Lizard Lady take money?"

"How much have you got?" Jackson asked from his horizontal posture.

She did a quick mental calculation. "With my and Jimmy's emergency money, about a hundred and fifty-five dollars."

"Hawth and I can throw in another hundred. Maybe Lilith will buy it." He didn't sound convinced.

This didn't make any sense. "I thought *we* were the buyers?"

"Mostly, Lilith covets stuff money can't buy. Like the magical moonstone. Which you are not giving her," he emphasized.

"Don't worry. I left it with Miriam for safekeeping." Morgan's neck felt empty without it.

"Good." He angled his head at Hawthorne. "We may have to let the egg go."

Hawthorne jerked as if Jackson had suggested he donate an arm. "No. Not that."

"Wait—what egg?" Jimmy pounced, voicing Morgan's question.

"I suppose you'll find out sooner or later." Hawthorne pointed dramatically at the floor. "Several stories below us in the cellar, tucked in a very large crate Jackson and I built and lined with hay, is a thunderbird egg."

"Incubating, even as we speak," Jackson affirmed. "The temperature is warm enough down there with the wood stove, but not hot enough to cook it. We've covered the egg with a blanket to mimic the mother bird sitting on top of it."

The astonishment in Jimmy's face mirrored Morgan's amazement. "Why?" he asked, speaking for them both.

Hawthorne had a mulish tilt to his chin. "To raise, after it hatches, and train our way."

"Awesome!" Jimmy sprang to his feet and gyrated in a dance. "Like training a dragon. Can I ride it?"

Hawthorne rubbed his chin. "I hadn't considered. Maybe."

"This is so cool." Jimmy jumped up and down like a character in a *Peanut's* cartoon strip. Or Calvin, of *Calvin and Hobbes* fame.

Morgan tried to wrap her mind around the staggering possibilities. "What do you want it to do, attack Panteras?"

A possessive glint lit Hawthorne's eyes. "Them too. It'd make a great watchbird. Thunderbirds imprint on the first thing they see, so I want it to be us. Not that wicked witch. The chick is due to hatch any day now."

The super-psyched kid hadn't stilled his feet. "How'd you get the egg, Hawth? Isn't it too late in the year for females to lay?"

"Their nesting period is longer than for other birds, and this was her second nest of the season. Jackson and I scaled a cliff two months ago and lifted it from the late clutch of eggs while the mama was off hunting."

"Oh, man." Jimmy radiated hero-worship. "I can totally picture you guys doing that."

So could Morgan. "But it will be too cold outside for a hatchling to survive. Even one this large. The mama will probably shepherd its siblings farther south."

"Probably," Jackson agreed, still prone on his back. "I'm hoping Grandma Miriam and Aunt Willow won't mind the baby flying around inside the lodge for a while."

"We'd feed the bird, and clean up after it, of course," Hawthorne added.

"Of course," Morgan echoed, although their hygienic standards weren't as high as the women's, given the state of this room. There might be some reason to the madness, though. A trained thunderbird could be a boon.

Another possible perk occurred to her. "Maybe it will eat that pesky owl." She and the unblinking bird that roosted in the main room of the lodge weren't the best of friends.

"Oh no." Hawthorne's brow arched. "We'd make certain they're OK together. Mom and Aunt Miriam love that demented owl. You're stuck with him."

"Great." Morgan's twitching tail reminded her of a

more pressing matter. "Even if you were willing to part with the egg," which she couldn't imagine they would be, "how are you transporting one that size? The pickup's not back yet."

Jackson's father and Hawthorne's mom and dad left early morning in the truck to get supplies from town, several hours away. They'd even hitched on the trailer for added provisions, an uncommon occurrence with these mostly self-sufficient people. They were stocking up for winter.

"One of the problems involved in moving it," Jackson conceded.

"And I don't want to let the egg go," Hawthorne repeated.

"Neither do I, when it comes right down to it. And the chick might not survive." Jackson smacked a fist into his palm. "The heck with it. We'll just have to gather our funds and shove the cash under her nose, the grasping lizard. Maybe even *insist* a little."

A fight breaking out with the Lizard Lady was daunting. Morgan shifted her gaze between the two guys. "Is there nothing else we can barter?"

Another fist smack from Jackson. "Nothing we'd want Lilith to have."

Hawthorne smiled a secret smile. "Maybe I can charm Dilly into getting what we need."

Jackson snorted, rolled off the bed, and stretched. "Even if Dilly is as taken with you as you think, she'd never go against that witch of a mother, and big sister Eve would betray her in a heartbeat. Something sinister about that one." He dropped his gaze to Morgan, still sunk on the beanbag. His eyebrows shot up. "What in God's name are you wearing?"

She smiled slightly. "Wondered when you'd notice."

He eyed her up and down. "Where did the clothes come from?"

"Not Wally world. Your grandma. Miriam."

"I've never seen her in that stuff before." He swiped a hand across his forehead. "She must've had it hidden away."

"Yeah." A flush heated Morgan's cheeks under his close inspection. "I look like I'm from another planet. And don't you suggest one, Jimmy."

"I wasn't," he protested. "Can't think of any that fit."

"Swell. I've even stumped Batboy."

The ghost of a smile flickered at Jackson's lips. "You're lovely. Truly. Allow me to assist you to your feet, my lady."

Despite everything, the canine ears, tail, and all the uncertainty, her fears diminished and her heart rate doubled at his gallantry. Warmth washed through her as she took his hand and rose, not easily done in skirts that tended to wrap around her ankles. Without his help, she might've sprawled on her face. Not the look she was going for—like any of this was.

Her arm linked through Jackson's, she turned with him to discover Miriam framed in the doorway. How long had she been standing there?

"Here." Miriam held out a tiny, ruby red glass phial, glowing like a jewel. "Save your money. Lilith won't want it from Wapicoli's."

"What about Morcants?" Morgan asked.

A shake of Miriam's head made her feathered earrings sway. "We'd rather she didn't learn that about

21

you. This is the nectar of a thousand honeysuckle blossoms blended with the juice of wild strawberries that grow in a secret spot along the creek bank. Lilith can't resist my special elixir."

"Neither can Okema," Hawthorne said under his breath.

"He'll have to go without this time. I make one batch a year." Miriam's hearing bordered on the psychic.

Even sealed, Morgan inhaled the fruity essence of the elixir. The sweet scent emanated through the cork, and her keen nose didn't miss a thing.

Miriam motioned to her. "You wish to know of those clothes?"

Her stomach fluttering, she nodded.

"They came from your Grandma Sarah."

Only Jackson's support kept her from staggering back. "What? How?"

"Sarah Morgan had a trunk of her belongings delivered to the lodge after her death in 1816 with instructions to save them for the Seventh Morcant. They've been hidden away here ever since. Waiting. For you."

Goosebumps pebbled Morgan from head to toe. Sarah had died two hundred years ago, and anticipated her coming. "Why didn't you tell me about this before?"

"You didn't need to know yet." Miriam held up a hand to halt any argument. "There's more."

"What? Grandma Sarah already gave me the moonstone."

"A gown or two for dressy wear. Some bits and pieces from the past, and a sealed letter for you. Read it after you return from seeing—or not seeing—Lilith."

Speechless, she simply nodded, and took the crimson vial Miriam extended.

"You tell Lilith, for me, that this nectar had better be enough." Miriam's tone was as ironclad as her gaze.

Morgan's three companions also stared after the older woman as she turned away, silver hair flowing down her back, beaded skirt catching the candlelight. "And I know about that egg, boys," she added, over her shoulder. "As does Willow. Yes, you may keep it," she said, waving aside their query before they even asked. "But see you do clean up after the creature and train it well. And heaven help us all, if you neglect to feed it enough."

Chapter Three
Off to See the Lizard

As the afternoon advanced, gray clouds banked over the ridges with the promise of rain. Cold drizzle misted the four of them gathered in the yard of the lodge before heading out on their quest—*The Three Musketeers and D'Artagnan.*

Or not. Jackson, Hawthorne, Jimmy, and especially Morgan were an unlikely comradeship, to say the least. But the musketeer's motto still applied: "All for one, and one for all." They'd battle to the death for each other.

Two weeks ago, Morgan wouldn't have considered herself a candidate for this pack. Scarcely even that many days had passed since she'd first fled to these mountains. In this brief window of time, the landscape had changed dramatically, as had she.

Like a song piping beauty and then gradually fading away, the splendors of autumn were gone with the wind. The chilly blast tore the remnants of the once glorious foliage from inky branches silhouetted in the haze. Where a fairy world had reigned, brushed with every hue in the artist's palette, swirling leaves now spilled over the ground. The colorful sea covered drifts of fern browned by frost and small purple asters braving a last blossom. Rocks and roots concealed in the leafy tide would require caution to navigate on the cloudy trail, but hike it she must.

If she were having this much difficulty with 'Wandering Wolf' already, what might the next full moon bring? Thank heavens for wise Miriam and the long dead grandmother reaching out to her from centuries' past. The unpredictable chief was in his secret warrior mode, his location a mystery.

She surveyed her companions from beneath the white cap and hooded green cloak. "Who'd have thought I'd be hiking to the Mountain Witch outfitted by Grandma Sarah?"

"Not me." Jimmy squinted at her, the hood of his rain jacket cinched under his reddened face. An outgrown sweatshirt of Hawthorne's hung to his knees below the outer layer. "Or anyone else making the trek to a lizard shifter with a nor'easter bearing down on us."

"Maybe the worst of the rain will hold off until our return." She hoped.

"I wouldn't count on it." The kid was a walking weather report.

"I'm not." She searched Jackson's somber gaze. He'd pulled his long black hair into a ponytail beneath the dark brown fedora, kind of an *Indiana Jones*/warrior/cowboy look. Leather pants molded his long legs above the boots.

Man, she wished the two of them could spend this wet day snuggled together by the fireside. "How far to Lilith's place?"

The edges of his mouth crimped, then he parted his lips. "Five miles, as the crow flies."

"Wish we were flying." Jimmy's eyes brightened above his rosy cheeks. "I can't wait until we get that thunderbird trained."

"Heck yeah," Hawthorne seconded, moisture dripping from the wide brim of a hat similar to Jackson's.

"It's not even hatched yet, and we've never attempted this with thunderbirds before," Jackson cautioned.

Hawthorne leaned in. "We've trained hawks, owls, and crows. Probably similar."

Jimmy nodded like a bobblehead. "I'll bet it is. Don't harsh my mellow, dude," he reproached Jackson. "That's a lot more birds than most people have worked with."

"OK." Jackson flung up a hand in concession. "We may train your dragon yet." He motioned for them to listen. "Stay close and alert. With luck, we'll return by evening. Not drag back in at night."

He singled out Morgan. "If we must fight, human form allows use of the weapons. But with full or partial change we can draw on the sheer power of the wolf. Determine for yourself which is better, or await my signal. Never fully change indoors, though."

This piece of advice puzzled her. "Why?"

"Wolves can't open doors. You may become trapped before making your escape."

"Unless I'm there to open it for you." Jimmy's android-like mind didn't miss a thing.

"Even then," Jackson argued. "Something could go wrong. And by *could*, I mean probably *will*."

"Right. No changing indoors. Assuming I have any say in the matter." She was doubtful.

"The very reason we're seeking out Lilith." Jackson slipped the bow strap over the shoulder of his chestnut-brown leather coat, and stepped out in front.

Morgan fell in behind him. Jimmy followed at her heels, and Hawthorne brought up the rear. They made their way through the windswept trees, the woodsy scent of plants and forest animals on the damp breeze. Each of them cast glances from side-to-side at the shrouded landscape. Hawthorne watched their backs.

He and Jackson were armed with bows and arrows, sheathed knives on one side of their belts, and tomahawks slung on the other. A slingshot similar to the kind used by the earliest Indians on the continent rode in the buckskin pouches at their waists. Guns had been declared too loud by Okema and were avoided by Wapicoli warriors gliding through the forest. These traditional weapons were effective and handcrafted.

Jimmy was armed with everything Jackson and Hawthorne had, minus the tomahawk. Given her irregular circumstances, Morgan had left all weapons behind except the potentially lethal scarf around her neck. The pebbles sewn into the end of the length of wool made it an effective defense to whip out.

As Jimmy had said, 'she could whack the daylights out of someone.' If Mateo or one of the other Panteras showed up, they just might be that someone.

The drizzle increased to a steady beat. Leaves were slick underfoot as they trudged over the foggy trail. Conditions could only worsen. A wolf wouldn't mind the wet so much, or would have the sense to seek shelter. Cold rain blowing in her face wasn't pleasant. There was nothing for it, though, other than to forge ahead.

"Onward ho," Morgan muttered. "We may need a boat."

"We should have the gear fishermen wear on *Deadliest Catch*." Batboy could convert miles to knots in a nanosecond. Nautical shows held particular appeal for him.

"Heavy yellow slickers?" Hawthorne asked.

"Some are orange and cover their legs, too," Jimmy pointed out. "We need to suit up from head-to-toe."

Hawthorne snorted. "Not exactly camouflage. We're being stealthy, remember?"

"Like anyone can see us in this washout, anyway. Heck, I can't even see us," Jimmy shot back.

Jackson hissed for quiet, but the bulk of the exchange was lost in the bluster whipping Morgan's skirts. Fortunately, the weight of the cloth and the cloak reaching to her ankles kept them from billowing too wildly. The last thing she wanted was her tail showing.

Well, *almost* the last thing. An attack by Panteras would be worse.

Strangely, the tail helped her keep her balance on the trail. She hoped the canine nose wouldn't reassert itself. In these clothes, she really would resemble the wolf disguised as the grandmother in *Little Red Riding Hood*. Her ability to control the ice queen was lessening, not improving.

Even if she could undo the change and be a 'normal' girl, though, she doubted she would. Control was one thing; losing her inner wolf entirely, quite another. At one with the rhythms of the earth, she rocked with the evergreen boughs and inhaled the damp forest scent, one hundred times stronger now than in her pre-wolf days. Her hearing, sight, every sense was heightened.

The helpless girl chased here by Mateo no longer existed. Good riddance. She simply wanted control.

Emotions coursed through her: Wonder at the connection with Grandma Sarah, excitement, and an equal measure of fear concerning her present challenge and what lay ahead. There was no choice other than to proceed with their plan and pray it worked. If the wolf fully took her over, Lord only knew what she might do, maybe ignite the war Okema had predicted between the Panteras and Wapicoli.

If she did, would they win?

He'd prophesied she would bring about the salvation or the ruin of the Wapicoli. Their fate hung in the balance, and she was the pendulum that would swing them one way or the other. She fervently prayed to be on the side of good.

Surely, if she wanted to do right badly enough, she would?

\*\*\*\*

"There." Gesturing for them to stop, Jackson halted behind a gnarled tree trunk covered with lichens. He pointed through the rain at the clearing cloaked in whiteness. "Stay on your guard. The giants could be anywhere."

His caution was barely audible above the wind, even with Morgan's sharp hearing. She recalled the brutes he'd referred to as giants who ran moonshine for Lilith, and the permission granted by Okema for him and Hawthorne to deal with the rednecks as they deemed necessary. No holds barred.

The giants must be human, but major badass. Dispatching nonhumans didn't require the nod from Okema. Apparently, the same rule applied to nosy government agents, one of whom was buried behind the lodge with Panteras and enemy werewolves. Okema had his own rules; when it came to the Wapicoli his word was law. Morgan endeavored to stay on the right side of the unfathomable chief.

Movement up ahead caught her eye. Scarcely more than a shadow in the mist and rain.

"What's that?" she whispered.

Jackson bent his head nearer hers. "A Pantera slipping into the woods. He's not our mission. We're letting him go this time. Understand?"

"Yes." They had pressing priorities.

She joined the others scanning the foggy site scattered with bare trees, milkweed pods, and grass poking through the sea of fallen leaves. A tangle of brush grew among the junked pickups that would never run again. Why people hung onto these derelict vehicles, she couldn't imagine. Parts, she supposed, for the one working truck, assuming it ran.

Everything that could go to seed had, including the two-story wood house encircled with tendrils of smoke from the chimney. The tang of hickory logs burning in the hearth and the meaty aroma of stew rode on the wind. Her empty stomach growled.

"Don't sample anything Lilith offers you." Jackson must've overheard her hunger pangs.

"Dilly wouldn't poison us." Hawthorne swiped his muddy boots on the patch of moss covering the knobby tree roots as if smartening himself up before heading inside. "She's different."

"Trust her at your peril," Jackson warned.

Hawthorne bristled and his hazel eyes turned neon green, like kryptonite. "I'm telling you she's not like the others."

Disapproval radiated from Jackson and his narrow gaze grew molten. "I'm not about to risk you discovering she is and having to pick up the pieces."

No fangs were bared—yet—but Hawthorne curled his lips. "I swear, Jackson. You're such a know-it-all."

He drew himself up to his full height, several inches taller than Hawthorne. "I'm trying to keep us all alive and *unhypnotized* as I promised Grandma Miriam. Your mother would also thank me. Not to mention our fathers, the clan, Okema…"

"I get it. No one likes Dilly. Except me," Hawthorne muttered.

"I might. I haven't met her yet." Morgan tried to run interference. She nudged Jimmy. "He might too."

"Sure," the kid fumbled, clearly not inclined to entertain the possibility of conviviality with the daughter of the infamous gorgon witch.

Jackson dipped fiery eyes to Morgan's. "Keep the interaction with Dilly to a minimum."

"Yeah. Wouldn't want her to eat you. Oh, wait. *We*'re the ones with that power." Hawthorne dripped sarcasm.

Jackson rumbled dangerously. "Don't test me, Hawth."

"Or what?" He crossed both arms over his chest.

Heels dug in, they stood glaring at each other. If push came to shove Morgan knew who'd win, but they'd lose precious time in foolish combat between them and weaken their defenses. A united front was vital.

Likely, the temperamental musketeers had their off days, too. She appealed to the incensed cousins. "Truce, guys?"

"If Hawth summons an ounce of sense," Jackson hissed.

He glowered at him. "You don't understand what it's like to be in love with someone you can't have."

"No?" Jackson's jaw jutted out. "If we don't help Morgan overcome the Wandering Wolf thing, I may never 'have' her. Any hope of our future together—the fate of us all—depends on the outcome of this visit. Don't for a moment forget who she is. Lilith won't, if she figures it out." His lava-filled gaze bored into Hawthorne's. "You've heard the prophecy. You know what the arrival of the seventh Morcant means."

Hawthorne's bulldog demeanor lessened slightly, and he gave a grudging nod. "Yes."

Chills darted down Morgan's spine at the grim reminder.

"Then we shall do as we must," Jackson summed up in true alpha style.

"Agreed." Despite his lingering reluctance, Hawthorne retook his position in the pack, a step behind his acknowledged leader.

With the squabble resolved, at least, temporarily, Jackson turned his focus to the hazy clearing. "That hellhole is where we're headed. May God have mercy on our souls if the she-devil outwits us."

His dire warning was a stark contrast to the seemingly innocuous house sprawling before Morgan. Her artistic eye noted the main section of the structure rose higher than the lower level and had been built earlier in traditional A-frame lines with a graded tin roof. The white paint applied long ago was chipped and faded, and the roof rusty. Even so, remnants of charm bore witness to the craftsmanship of the builder who'd designed his mountain home in a protected hollow.

The addition to the original house resembled a cabin tagged onto the left-hand side. A wooden porch ran the entire length of the front with pieces of tin missing from its roof. Chairs lined the porch. Was one of them the bench seat from a pickup?

Looked like it, but she couldn't be sure. The blankets and comforters hanging over the porch railing blocked her view. "Why all the laundry on a rainy day?"

"Lilith signals when her latest batch of shine is ready by the amount of wash on the line," Jackson explained over his shoulder. "I'd say she's expecting a brisk trade."

Morgan tried to make sense of the arrangement. "So, she sells directly from her home and also delivers?"

"Right. The giants are probably out making the rounds now. Once someone has tasted her shine, they're a regular."

"Why?" Morgan imagined men thumping their chests after knocking back the fiery brew, barely able to croak their appreciation. "Has she got some special ingredient to make the stuff irresistible?"

"Yeah. Enchantment. She spells the stuff."

"Ah." Morgan got it now. "Guarantees sales."

"Exactly. Doesn't matter what she makes as long as she tempts you with that first swallow." Rain dripped steadily over the back of Jackson's fedora and down his leather coat as he spoke, wetting the bow and arrows in the quiver.

Not that it mattered in his, or anyone else's, ability

to fire. Unless their fingers were too numb. Dang, Morgan was chilled to her toes. The raw wet seeped through her wool wrappings and she wished this home offered hospitality, not grave danger. In the early days, it probably did.

Jimmy pressed past her for a better look. "What about revenuers? Don't they go after people selling moonshine?"

Jackson chuckled as if the kid had made a joke. "Like they'd ever live to tell the tale."

"Yeah," Hawthorne scoffed. "Never make it out alive."

"Why? Has Lilith turned them all to stone?" Jimmy's query reminded Morgan of the white witch in the *Chronicles of Narnia*.

"Near enough. The ones allowed to escape work for *her* now. The disappearance of the rest remains a mystery, as far as the government's concerned." Jackson nodded at the ample female figure coming through the front door, the bulk of her hidden by the blankets on the rail. "Well, there she is, the Lizard Lady herself. Though no 'lizarding' tonight. She can't bask in moonlight with this cloud cover."

The witch creeped Morgan out even more than Mateo did, which said a lot. "Does that diminish her power?"

Jackson swiveled toward her. "I wouldn't count on it."

Annoyance roiled in her alongside the fear. "Why do people keep saying that to me?"

He waved aside her indignation. "Because it's true. Only means she can't shift."

"As far as we know," Hawthorne amended.

Morgan huddled in her damp cloak. "Cripes, guys. You're not making this any easier."

"That's a big ten-four," Jimmy agreed.

"Never said it was a fun outing." Jackson took her arm. "Get your safety glasses on, Wolf Girl. It'll be hard for you to see with everything in reverse from the mirrors. I'll guide you to Lilith's lair. Still got that precious nectar from Grandma Miriam safely tucked away?"

"Here." She patted the pocket sewn inside her cloak where she'd secreted the ruby vial for the all-important barter. It rested against her chest.

"Good." Jackson's lips twitched in a slight smile. "Put on those night vision goggles, Jimbo. We're off to see the lizard."

A snort-laugh escaped Jimmy at his play on words.

Morgan didn't think it was funny.

Chapter Four
The Lizard Lady's Lair

Water cascaded over the porch roof where the four of them stood dripping. Usually, rain drumming on a tin roof ranked among the most relaxing sounds in the world. Not now. Morgan wasn't the only one summoning courage before they knocked to gain entry.

"Holy moly, what's up with that door?" The stout oak appeared as if somebody, or multiple bodies, had slashed at the wood and beaten it repeatedly with a hammer.

Jackson bent nearer. "Maybe the *regulars* demanding refills of Lilith's moonshine when she's running low."

Hawthorne ran his fingers over the deep groves. "That's the trouble with enchanted brews, insatiable customers."

"Some of whom tried to claw their way in. Wonder if the other side of the wood is equally marked from attempts to get out?" Morgan wouldn't be at all surprised.

"'Abandon hope all ye who enter here.'" Jimmy kept his voice low, but loud enough to be heard above the wind and rain. They were all mindful of their voices carrying.

Morgan shivered despite her wrappings. Derelict chairs and the bench seat from the pickup flanked them on either side. "At least we're out of the worst of the weather for the moment."

Batboy turned his bug-eyed night vision goggles on her. "Small comfort, considering we could all be *petrified* if we look into those lizard eyes. It's kind of like entering the *Chamber of Secrets.*"

A shudder ran through her. "It really is. We need a portkey for a speedy exit." She was extra vulnerable having to face backwards to see what was in front of her through the mirrors. "Is anyone, say Lilith, watching us? It's mega creepy wondering."

Jackson swiveled his head. "Not that I can tell."

"I'll double-check." Jimmy adjusted his goggles, making that night vision sound, and scanned the premises. "Alpha Charlie reporting perimeter clear."

"Where has our lizard gotten to?" Dwindling daylight and the foggy rain further blurred Morgan's wonky sight.

"She's probably out back checking her still. It's kept locked in what's practically a bunker," Jackson explained.

"Reckon she's got any giants with her?" Morgan wasn't eager to meet with the brutes.

"One generally guards the still. Don't worry. We'll be okay. Everyone just do as we agreed." Despite Jackson's insistence, he didn't exude confidence.

Uneasiness coupled with misery brought out the whiner in Morgan. "Why couldn't we be dropping in on someone normal? Kick back and eat dinner, watch some TV, you know, what regular people do?"

Again, the bug-eyed surveillance from batboy. "Are you freaking kidding me? Standing here with wolf ears and a tail hidden under our colonial grandmother's clothes?"

Hawthorne slapped his hat against his side in a shower of droplets. "Nothing weird about that. Heck no."

"Face it, Morgan. No *normal* person would let us in their house to use the phone, let alone have dinner," Jimmy said.

"Exactly. Time to make her more presentable." Jackson gave her icy fingers a reassuring squeeze. "Ready, guys?"

She forced a casual reply. "Sure. I've got nothing better to do."

Jimmy nodded. "A slot in my busy schedule opened up."

"Date night for me." Hawthorne practically hummed with anticipation.

Ignoring his loony cousin, Jackson hammered on the door. After a few moments, the curtains at the dingy window on the first floor twitched. An instant later, the lock turned, and the door swung wide.

Morgan braced herself for *The Creature from the Black Lagoon*, but it wasn't Lilith. Whatever the Lizard Lady looked like, this girl was way too young. A teenager of fifteen or sixteen wearing tight jeans, tall leather boots, and a pink tank top gaped at them from the other side of the threshold.

*Who the heck?* Light from several lamps inside illuminated the onlooker, and Morgan's wolf vision was superior to a normal person's.

Color flushed the girl's petal fresh skin. Blue-green eyes outlined in smoky liner widened in a sweet oval face. A mass of auburn hair tumbled to her waist, covering most—not all—of the generous endowments her skimpy top didn't. If this was Dilly, Morgan understood Hawthorne's ardent attraction.

Their impromptu hostess overcame her initial shock. A smile curved sensuous lips glistening with gloss. "Hey Jackson. Good to see you."

"Hey Dilly."

She swept her gaze over the assembly on the porch, seeking a particular face. "Hey Hawthorne."

"Hey Dilly." A buzz of excitement underscored his reply, as if he'd added an unspoken term of endearment, like dearest Dilly, or darling Dilly, or will you be mine forever, Dilly?

She lifted her hand in a shy wave, which Hawthorne, no doubt, returned, but he was beyond Morgan's limited line of sight. The female pheromone Dilly emitted heightened upon seeing him, a reaction not lost on Morgan's acute sense of smell. He must be wowed. At this moment, she doubted he even remembered why they'd come.

Dilly gestured at the assembly on her doorstep. "Who are your friends, Jackson?" she asked, addressing the leader of the pack for pertinent information.

He motioned to the two newcomers. "This is Morgan and her brother, Jimmy." He omitted their last name. "They're staying at the lodge."

With that brief explanation, Dilly must content herself. Apparently, she did. The next thing Morgan knew, Dilly was motioning them inside.

"Hey y'all. Good to meet you. Come on in," she beckoned, with down-home friendliness. "You must be soaked to the skin. Terrible day to be out. Not that you aren't used to it. Even so." She paused in her onrush, sliding her questioning gaze at Morgan, then back to

Jackson. "Are you wanting me to fetch Mama?"

"Yes, thank you. If you'd kindly get her for us, please." He was in polite mode with Dilly.

"Sure. Happy to. I'll go right now. Make yourselves comfy." She cast a wistful smile at Hawthorne that must've scored big time with the lovesick boy, then pivoted and disappeared toward the other end of the house.

Morgan couldn't tell if Jackson had met Dilly's eyes, but she'd bet Hawthorne had full on. Maybe the girl was harmless enough and had escaped her mother's unfortunate attributes. She seemed genuinely nice and eager to please. Morgan pitied the unlucky couple with so much against them, and prayed they didn't turn out like *Romeo and Juliet*—that hadn't ended well.

"Come on. Hope we don't regret this." Jackson steered Morgan through the front door into the room. Awkward to accomplish backwards.

"I already do. Whew—" she broke off, choking on the cloud of smoke.

A heat wave hit her from the big black stove crouched across the room like a live thing, dominating one wall. Ash from the grate liberally sprinkled the floor, pockmarked with burns, in front of the antiquated monstrosity. Chunks of kindling piled to the side of the stove provided a steady supply to feed the ravenous beast. Not only did it belch—the chimney needed sweeping—but the pall of cigarette smoke hung in the air. She craved warmth, however, werewolves couldn't tolerate as much heat as regular people, and the smoke would do anyone in.

Jackson muffled a cough. "Won't take long to thaw, assuming we don't suffocate."

"Holy inferno, Batman—" A coughing fit halted Jimmy. "Should've worn a hazmat suit."

"Does Lilith's reptilian blood require the furnace of Hades? No wonder Dilly's in a tank top." If Morgan stayed beyond the time needed to feel her toes, she'd shed clothes fast. But there was only so far she dared go, or she'd be down to her tail.

"I prefer Dilly that way." Hawthorne was the least affected of them all, likely in a world of his own.

"I'll bet," Jackson said acidly, "probably too head-over-heels to notice little things like the cloud of poisonous smoke or our imminent incineration."

"Red alert, red alert. Engines on overload, captain." Jimmy sounded the alarm in his Trekkie voice.

"Noted, Ensign Chekhov," Jackson indulged him.

"Commander," Jimmy corrected. "But I'll let it go."

Jackson smiled faintly. "Good of you."

"Are we supposed to sit or stand while awaiting the explosion?" Morgan wondered aloud.

Jackson didn't make a move, not even to take off his hat. "I'd crouch in an open window and gulp in air, if that was an option."

Jimmy swept an expansive arm at the room. "I'd take the escape pod and jettison out of here."

"You would." Morgan swiveled her head at their surroundings. The place was an absolute dump. What Lilith did with the profits from her illegal enterprise was anyone's guess.

No outlay for an expensive rug, that's for sure. Puddles dripped at their feet and spread over the scuffed floor strewn with ashes. Stained wallpaper hung loose in places. Tape showed someone's failed efforts to secure those sections. Saggy couches and armchairs, stuffing showing in spots, were crammed together.

The glossy magazines heaped on a dusty coffee table surprised her. "No expense spared on this stash. There's enough magazines in here to furnish a doctor's waiting room. Orthodontists have the priciest kinds." She'd suffered through braces for her perfect bite.

Jimmy indicated the cartons of cigarettes. "No doctor would approve those."

"And no charity would take this furniture, even if it was offered. A junkyard, maybe, and they'd have to be paid. A lot," Morgan added.

"You guys are mighty snarky." Hawthorne paced, his boots squeaking on the floor, as if in expectation of Dilly's return. "Sure, it's a smidge hot and smoky in here, but the room has a certain charm." He muted a cough with his sleeve. "And Morgan complained she was frozen not ten minutes ago."

"Hell warms a gal up." A light steam rose from her damp wrap in the tropical heat. She wrinkled her nose. "Dang it. I smell like a wet dog in this sodden wool. An unpleasant side effect of a wolf in sheep's clothing, I suppose."

Jimmy snorted. Jackson and Hawthorne chuckled, but Morgan was too tired and hungry, on top of everything else, to relish her wit. "Is there any end to this wretched day?"

Jackson laid his hand on her shoulder. "We're taking off the instant we accomplish our mission."

She had to get a grip. "Sorry for being such a *Debbie Downer*. I know you're all miserable too."

"I'm okay." Hawthorne swiveled periodically toward the door. "And hey, you wanted to watch some

TV." He drew her attention to big, boxy television on a tabletop ringed from innumerable cups of coffee and moonshine. Stacks of DVD's teetered beside it.

"Lilith or her girls are avid viewers." Morgan had a thought. "Say, is there a Mr. Dubois?"

"None I've ever heard of. Maybe she mates like a praying mantis and then eats the males." Jackson imitated a giant chomping insect.

Morgan jerked. "Makes you wonder, doesn't it?"

"Someone's been watching *Buffy* reruns," Hawthorne interjected.

"Feels like I'm in one. Does that make me the slayer?" She had the creeped out suspicion it did.

"Shhh—Lilith's coming." Hawthorne's footsteps slowed, his bravado fading.

A scent, frog maybe, veiled in cigarette smoke, accompanied the tread in the hall beyond the side door. Morgan could scarcely breathe, and not only because of the thick smog. The creature was nearly upon them. Would she have scales and webbed fingers with slashing claws, or coiling snake hair?

Surely, Jackson would've mentioned that.

"What are y'all doing standing around in here? Didn't Dilly invite you through to the kitchen for some coffee? I swear that girl'll forget her head next." On the tail of this hospitable drawl in a husky smoker's voice, a large woman emerged through the door. Rain beaded the reddish mane she'd pulled back with a scrunchy pink hair band. A fuzzy bathrobe of the same hue, belted at her wide waist, met the pink and black polka-dot splasher boots muddy from her trek to the still.

Morgan's first thought: *Crap!* She had an identical pair at Aunt M.'s townhouse in Woodstock. Well, no more. And her second thought: *What the freakin heck?* Lilith wasn't in the least as she'd expected.

*Seriously?* This was her usual attire? And what was with those eyes?

Instead of the emerald gaze Morgan had feared tumbling into like enticing pools of water, Lilith's green eyes were heavy-lidded and sleepy. No dark circles smudged her seemingly sleep deprived gaze, though. Maybe she always appeared this way, except when she was an actual lizard, of course.

A grin split Lilith's round face as she took in the visitors. "Oh, I see what's going on. A big bad wolf's been telling nasty stories about me. Shame on you, Jackson Wapicoli." Deep-throated laughter accompanied her scolding.

"What makes you think I said anything, Lilith?" His casual tone belied his rigid stance beside Morgan.

"Well, it wasn't that sweet Hawthorne. My apple pie Wapicoli boy."

If Lilith expected hugs and kisses in return, she was disappointed. Hawth bared his teeth—kind of like a dog Morgan used to have—in an ingratiating smile.

Still chuckling, she fixed her lazy eyes on Morgan. "Who knocked up those glasses for you, honey? Let me guess. The kid in the goggles." The barrel shaped woman doubled over with mirth. "It's too much," she sputtered between outbursts, waving plump fingers at Morgan and Jimmy. "And here I thought we were having a slow day."

"Glad we could entertain you," Jackson said icily.

She slapped her hefty sides. "Oh, you are, honey. You are. No wonder Dilly skittered off."

Hawthorne stepped forward. "Could I maybe have

a word with her?"

"Sure you can, sugar. In the kitchen." Lilith thumbed at the door. "Have some coffee and cinnamon buns."

"Hawth!" Jackson snapped.

"Just for a minute," he pleaded, and shot past them.

There wasn't anything Jackson could do about Hawthorne going AWOL except chase after him and abandon Morgan. He remained, but she sensed him simmering. He'd blow later.

One strange thing Morgan noticed concerning Lilith, no tears ran down her cheeks after her lapse into mirth. Her dry face was lined like parchment, but she couldn't be all that old. Could she? Not with a daughter Dilly's age. Was the appearance of her skin from excessive cigarettes and heat, or the reptilian factor? Both, maybe.

Morgan could hardly pose the question, nor point out that her aura was greenish black. Not a good thing—for them. Lilith probably didn't care her aura was the color of slime.

She observed Hawthorn's speedy exit, then slipped a pack of cigarettes and a lighter from the pocket on her robe. "Poor boy," she crooned, flicking the lighter. "He's got it bad for my Dilly. Not that I blame him. She's not the sharpest knife in the drawer, but pretty as a peach."

Jimmy cleared his throat. "Maybe, I'll go with Hawth—"

"Stay, goggle boy," Lilith rapped, newfound grit in her tone. "We got us some business to attend to and I think you figure in." She turned her eyes on Morgan, not the glittering green she'd expected, but unnerving.

Lilith rarely blinked.

Sisterly instinct to protect Jimmy gave her the oomph to battle the stifling intimidation. "Hold on. You don't need Jimmy. He's not involved."

"Oh, I disagree, honey." Lilith blew a smoke ring overhead.

Jackson shook his head. "We're not here to be dictated to by you."

Smoke trailing from her cigarette, Lilith waved at the door. "If you have no need of my services, go. But I expect you do, or you wouldn't have come."

Jimmy gave Morgan a thumb's up. "It's OK, guys. We can stay."

Arms crossed, Jackson stood his ground. "For now."

Satisfaction crossed Lilith's intent gaze. "As I expected."

It wasn't lost on Morgan that she watched each of them—but especially her—all the time. Her skin crawled under the fixity of that scrutiny.

"Well then, let's see what we're dealing with." A creepola smile playing over her face, Lilith slowly circled Morgan.

*Always keep the shifter in sight.*

Was the ice queen speaking to her? Uncertain, but forewarned, Morgan rotated with Lilith, watching her through the flip down mirrors. Tricky to do. Lilith was surprisingly agile for a woman of her size, and she increased the speed.

*Look deeper. She's not just a woman.*

Again, the inner voice directed Morgan.

Round and round they turned, Morgan searching the broad face, and lazy, heavy-lidded eyes. *Dizzying.*

46

She grew uncomfortably warm, even panting. Not Lilith. Rather like a cat tormenting a mouse, and Morgan was definitely not the serene feline in this scenario.

"What's your game, Lilith?" Jackson growled.

"Don't get those sleek britches in a knot, honey. Look better on you as they are. I'm just checking out your girlfriend." She stopped and tilted her head to one side. "What's the matter, honey? You got wolf troubles?"

Alarm sharpened in Morgan. How did she know?

"Oh, I know a lot, sweetie."

*Great. A mind reader.*

A smug smile curved her lips. "Sure am. We don't even have to talk out loud to have this conversation. You want what's in my pocket?"

Morgan was wary, Jackson ready to spring, and Jimmy rolled behind a chair in combat mode as Lilith withdrew a small emerald flask from her fuzzy robe.

Giving a short laugh, she held the tincture high. The bottle glinted venomously in the light. "Y'all are mighty jumpy. Course, if I let this stuff loose in here, you'd all be dead, unless goggle boy, back there, has a gasmask on him."

"Never without it," Jimmy muttered, but Morgan knew he'd left it behind at the townhouse. No matter how super prepared batboy was, he could only fit so much into his backpack.

Lilith gave a short laugh. "Don't worry, kid. The stopper stays on. I ain't immune to this potion either. But a wee bit doled out by that smart Miriam Wapicoli and your sister will do just fine." She honed in on Morgan again. "You got too much wolf in you, don't you, gal?"

"A tad." She tried to block further insights into her mind.

Triumph gleamed in Lilith's unwavering gaze. "What'd you bring me? Jackson knows I love goodies."

"We've got what you want. Grandma says to tell you it had better be enough for the barter," he added firmly.

A look that could only be described as respect shadowed Lilith's eyes. "If you brought me what I think you did. It's enough for *this* trade."

His tension was palpable. "What do you mean?"

Shrugging as if it made no difference to her, she held out the green vial. "Let's swap, then chat some more."

Morgan dipped trembling fingers into her inner pocket and closed them around the precious bottle. She pulled it out, the sweet red nectar shining with invitation.

An appreciative glint flickered in Lilith's keen regard. "That's the stuff."

"Yours first." Jackson extended his hand. She deposited the sought-after cure in his palm, and he tucked it into the buckskin pouch at his waist. "Now, Morgan."

At his direction, she transferred the ruby vial to Lilith, recoiling at the clammy feel of her skin.

"So far, so good." Lilith acted amenable enough, but something about her struck a chord of dread in Morgan, and Jackson remained rigid. Jimmy still crouched behind the chair.

"There's just one more thing," their unlikely hostess continued. "Something I've wanted for a long time. I think you could help me get it, Wolf Girl."

Jackson rumbled warning in his chest. "Why should she?"

Victory flickered in her unblinking eyes. "Because she's gonna need my help again."

"What for? We have an agreement. You want Miriam angered? How about Okema?" He growled their names.

Lilith stilled. He'd hit a nerve.

"No need to trouble them. Let's keep this between us," she wheedled, pressing near Morgan.

Instinctively, she turned away. The next thing she knew, Lilith was on the opposite side of her. How had she moved *that* quickly?

Again, Morgan turned, and Lilith was in front, then at her back. A snarl on his lips, Jackson whipped around to stay between them. No matter what he did, or how Morgan rotated, Lilith was there. She was *every freaking where*. It didn't help that Jackson had to watch her like a sheepdog. Lilith had them at a disadvantage, and the hoarse laugh rang out louder and louder.

If Morgan hadn't fully grasped it before, she did now. Lilith was wicked to the core, the deceptively sleepy look a pretense, to put them off their guard. Like a seemingly idle lizard suddenly snaking out its long tongue and snatching a fly, she'd snared them.

A familiar whirring caught her ears. Jimmy swung the leather thong of his slingshot, the one used by warriors for a millennium. Lilith flinched as a small stone thwacked her on the side of the head, breaking her concentration. Morgan was amazed he'd had the presence of mind to attack, but the kid was unflappable. He must've readied himself from his hiding place, then sprang into action.

He positioned another stone in the sling. "Get out of here, Morgan!"

"Not yet, you little brat." Lilith was on him at lightning speed. She jerked the slingshot from his hand and the goggles off his head. Before Morgan or Jackson could stop her, she'd trapped his cheeks in her hands, tilted his face toward hers, and gazed deeply into his unwilling eyes.

"You cheating bitch!" Jackson roared.

Morgan's mouth opened in horror. "What have you done to him?"

Lilith dropped her hands. Jimmy wore a dazed expression. Smoke encircled him as the witch contemplated Morgan. "You'll never know, unless you do as I bid."

Rage rushed through Morgan. If lightning had struck her, the fiery current couldn't be stronger. "I'll tear your head off unless you free him from whatever spell you just cast!"

Jackson's glowing eyes reflected the inferno in Morgan, but he hesitated. "Maybe we should hear her out first, Morgan."

Lilith straightened. "That's right. Listen to your pack leader."

Snarls rose in Morgan's throat and she bared her teeth—now fangs. "He's not *my* leader, crone! I'm a Morcant! Do you know what that means?"

The faintest flicker touched Lilith's unswerving gaze. "For your baby brother's sake, sweetie, hear me out."

Thinking past the red haze fogging her mind was nearly impossible. "Oh, you'll talk, or you'll die!"

Chapter Five
The Ice Queen Unleashed

"Wait!" Jackson threw out an arm to stop Morgan from attacking Lilith.

The power crackling through her intensified. She easily shoved him aside and tore past. He was no longer dealing solely with Morgan.

Lilith flashed out of reach.

Again, Morgan lunged at her. Again, she missed.

"You think to fight me, Wolf Girl. In those ridiculous spectacles?" she taunted.

*Take them off*, commanded the inner voice. *Set me free.*

Morgan came to an immediate decision. She ripped off the glasses, with Jackson yelling, "Don't! It's what she wants!" and sent them splintering to the floor.

Jimmy shook his head, as if waking from a dream. "Take these!" He tossed Morgan the goggles.

She let them fall. She hadn't fully changed yet, but her fingernails were claws and her hands white with fur. The ears and tail were already evident. She patted her nose. Yep. The canine form was back. Loosing the wolf, like a hound from its chain, she howled her fury.

Lilith went on the offensive. Before Morgan opened a vein in her throat, she was face-to-face with those hooded eyes. "None can resist me. Not even you, Morcant girl," she crooned, zapping Morgan with the full force of her hypnotic rays.

*You will do as I say*, Lilith dictated.

A sense of helpless spiraling, not knowing where she was, only the droning in her head that must be heeded, and then—

*No!* Morgan snapped into the moment. The white-hot rage firing through her energized her beyond anything she'd ever known. A coiling vortex of power deep inside her pushed back against the mesmerizing bombardment. Blue light filled her mind with the brilliance of the stars, a sort of mental force field. The ice queen was shielding her, but it took everything she and her wolf self possessed for this all-out fight.

Surprise widened Lilith's heavy-lidded gaze. In that instant, Morgan hurled the larger woman into a couch and bent over her. "I'm not just any Morcant. I'm the Seventh!"

Lilith hadn't seen that coming. Supreme satisfaction coursed alongside the realization that Morgan needed help to block the powerful witch and maintain her hold. Fatigue from battling the ongoing rays, combined with the heat and fumes in the room, was taking its toll. But Jackson would have to risk that mind controlling gaze to get close enough to aid her.

Wait. What was she thinking? He was equally empowered—maybe more so—as the Seventh Wapicoli male and descendent of the Star People. He need only harness his birthright.

"Jackson! You can ward her off too!"

He flew to Morgan's side so swiftly the air around her whistled. Lilith was fast, but they were faster. Together, they seized her struggling bulk and forced her against the wall. Fierce protection for Jimmy drove

Morgan on. She closed half hands, half wolf paws around Lilith's thick throat. Finally. Those eyes blinked.

"Speak witch. What have you done to my brother?"

Lilith might be startled, but not defeated. A sneer curled her lips. "You have until the next full moon to complete the task I give you."

Morgan tightened her hold. "Or what?"

Strangling sounds accompanied her viselike grip. "Let her breathe," Jackson urged. "We have to know."

Being this close to the lizard was loathsome anyway. Morgan let go. "Say what you have to say. Then I'll tear your throat out."

Lilith's massive bosom heaved beneath her robe as she recovered her airflow. "Oh, I doubt that. Bring me the sea serpent's fang that hangs from the necklace around Santiago's neck, the leader of the Mountain Panteras."

"I know who he is," Morgan snarled.

"Good. Then you're up to speed. If I don't get the fang, Jimmy will—" Lilith paused, and snapped her fingers.

"Walk off a cliff on the next full moon," he said robotic style, eyes zombiefied.

Morgan stared at him in horror. "Jimmy, that's not funny."

"He's not joking." Lilith snapped her fingers again and he resumed a normal, albeit annoyed, face.

"I'm gonna fly back here on my thunderbird one day and have it peck your eyes out, witchy woman."

"Sure you will, baby cakes." She laughed. "Such an imagination." She targeted Morgan like a hunter sighting a deer. "The choice is yours. Bring me what I want or he falls to his death. The end."

She seethed to tear the lizard apart. "I could kill you now. Break the spell."

Lilith tossed her a scornful glance. "Only I can break the spell. Learn the drill, Number Seven. Jackson knows. All the Wapicoli know. Don't you?"

Heat inflamed his narrow glare, but he nodded. "Once the spell is cast only she can undo it."

"How sweet it is." Lilith smirked. "Better get your girlfriend in line before she does something you'll regret."

Morgan couldn't believe her ears. "Okema can counter her curse, can't he?"

Jackson lifted one broad shoulder and let it drop. If he knew, he wasn't saying.

Lilith frowned through a haze of smoke. After everything, she still had her blasted cigarette. "If you send that snake of a chief here I won't break the spell no matter what."

She might be bluffing. Morgan couldn't be certain. The threat hanging over Jimmy kept her from shredding the vile creature into minute pieces. Barely.

"Yeah? Maybe I'll stab you through the heart with that fang you—"

"Rein it in, Morgan. We're done here," Jackson bit out.

"But, Lilith—"

"Now!" he barked, in full alpha force. "Our business is concluded, for today."

Shock waves coursed through her, and she gaped at him, but backed down. He was right, much as she hated to admit it.

"Hawthorne! Get in here!" Jackson's bellow

reverberated through the house.

No reply.

He strode to the hall door, and flung it open. "Hawth! You better appear in the next two seconds or I'm leaving you here for good!"

Footsteps pounded down the stairs and into the hall. No stealthy Wapicoli tread this time. Hawthorne burst into the room, followed by Dilly. What the two had been doing, Morgan could only imagine. Both were flushed, although to give Hawthorne credit, he was still fully clothed.

Jackson eyed his cousin coldly. "Thanks for all your support."

"Sorry." He was a little breathless, adjusting his bow and arrows and his hat. "We didn't hear you over the CDs."

"How lame is that?" Jackson thrust back. "Not that we needed backup. Jimbo's just been cursed, that's all."

Hawthorne's jaw dropped.

Hands on her hips, Dilly advanced on her mother. "Why'd you go and do that for, Mama? I can't have any friends over without you spelling them."

She flicked cigarette ash in an overflowing tray on the coffee table. "Then don't. Who needs them?"

"I do. I'm sick to death of hanging out with drunks wasted out of their skulls, and the rest of those losers. I'm going off with Hawthorne to the lodge." She stamped her foot. "So there."

Hawthorne stood stock still while Jackson stared from one to the other. "Dilly, we can't show up at the lodge with you."

"Sure you can. Please, Jackson. I won't be any bother. Even help out with the chores. Mama will let me go stay awhile, won't you?" Lip quivering, she implored her irate parent.

Lilith waved her aside. "Makes no difference to me. Go ahead, useless girl. Eve's worth three of you any day. More."

The unkind comparison to her older sister stung. Tears glistening, Dilly turned away. "I'll grab my bag and coat."

"Wait. What?" Morgan asked. Had Dilly packed, or was she already planning to run off?

Swiping at her eyes, she pushed back lengths of reddish hair. "Living here, you have to be prepared to go."

Morgan didn't blame her, but watched in disbelief while the shaken girl tugged a large backpack out from behind the couch and snagged a parka from a hook behind the door.

"Ready!" Dilly cast a defiant glare at her mother and an imploring look at Jackson.

"Dilly, Okema may send you packing, or never even let you near the lodge," he warned.

"I'd rather take my chances with him, than her." She stabbed an accusing finger at Lilith.

She flicked more cigarette ash. "They're werewolves, honey. Or hadn't you noticed? You might get bit."

Shaking, but determined, Dilly squared her chin. "Hawthorne won't let anyone hurt me, will you?"

"No. Never." But his eyes didn't reflect his assurance.

He had to be thinking what they all were. *Dear Lord. Okema.*

"Jackson?" Again, Dilly entreated the pack leader

and future chief.

Morgan knew taking Dilly under his protection wasn't what he'd ever wanted. He'd made that abundantly plain before; the reluctance in his demeanor said it all now.

"Please?" Tears slid down her cheeks and quivering chin.

Groaning with the full knowledge of what bringing her home could mean, he nodded. "I'll do my utmost for you."

Relief lit her liquid gaze. "Thanks, Jackson. You're the best."

"Not so fast, sugar. You're not home free yet." Lilith pointed the cigarette at Morgan. "It's Wolf Girl here and that poisonous chief you have to worry about."

"I won't hurt her," Morgan fired back.

"No?" Lilith inhaled coolly and slowly exhaled. "What if she's a threat to that adored brother of yours?"

Morgan rounded on Dilly. "You're not, are you?"

"See there?" Lilith laughed at how quickly she'd turned.

"I'm not a threat to anybody," Dilly pleaded. "Mama just says mean stuff."

Lilith's secret smile instilled more doubt.

"Come on then. We are so gone." Jackson turned and strode across the room. Practically ripping the front door off its hinges, he banged it open and disappeared into the bluster. Morgan, and she suspected everyone else, followed him in a state of shock.

"I'll be waiting for my next goodie!" Lilith called after them, as if the threat branded on Morgan's brain wasn't enough. "And Dilly will come crawling back when Okema tosses her out. Unless he does worse, foolish girl!"

"I'll be back too! On my thunderbird!" Jimmy hurled at her.

"Can't wait! Ride 'em, cowboy!" A cackle followed them into the junkyard beyond the house.

No mere mortal could cackle that loudly. Not in this wind. Lilith was having the final word and last laugh.

*Not next time*, Morgan vowed, gasping in the icy wet after the smoky inferno. Cold rain sheeted from a gray sky and mist veiled the darkening trees. Nightfall soon. The homeward march would be doubly wretched.

They never should've come. She'd endangered Jimmy seeking a cure for *Wandering Wolf*, likely put them all at risk. And nearly lost her mind in the process.

How they were getting the serpent's tooth from Santiago, she shuddered to think. The Mountain Panteras had their lair in a cavern. She didn't even know where it was. Surely, they had cabins, too, or a cluster of trailers, somewhere?

No idea, only the keen awareness that all Panteras, whether the mountain or city variety, were their mortal enemy.

What were they going to do? More importantly, how could she make this right for Jimmy?

In turmoil, she hastened after Jackson, wasting no time on his trek. Hawthorne straggled behind, helping Dilly on with her parka. Jimmy trotted at their heels.

"Jackson!" Morgan caught up to him on the muddy trail, unprepared for how much it sapped her dwindling strength. Panting, she clasped his arm.

He bent his head to speak with her above the roar in the woods. "That went well," he said gruffly.

"Yeah. Terrific. Okema won't bite Dilly, will he?"

"God only knows. I'll intercede for her, but Okema will do as he will do." The Wapicoli mantra.

"Okema has rules against harming humans, with rare exceptions, right?" Morgan reasoned.

"Yeah. But I'm not entirely sure she's fully human."

"Really?" She envisioned the tearful girl. "Dilly seems normal enough, and doesn't smell reptilian like her mother. What else would she be?"

"A witch. Might not even realize it herself yet." His tone was somber.

"Oh crap." The Wapicoli did not like witches. "Now what?"

Circling his arms around Morgan, he drew her against him. "Somehow, someway, we'll get through this."

She savored a stolen moment nestled close to him, and not only because of his tenderness, also for his welcome support. "You almost make me believe it."

A nagging conscience chided her. "About before, I'm sorry I defied you in front of Lilith."

"That's OK. You're not yourself."

"You can say that again." And her condition was worsening more rapidly than she cared to admit.

Was there no end to the ramifications of her curse?

Chapter Six
The Wolfward Pull

Heaven help her, Morgan was deteriorating at an alarming rate. The rain had finally stopped and bright stars twinkled through the dark branches tossing overhead, but the storm had slowed their retreat to the lodge. More wolf than woman now, she struggled to walk upright in the wet skirts whipping around her ankles.

*Dratted cloth.* She hated the stuff. If she could articulate the words out loud, she'd complain vehemently. Human speech was no longer possible, though.

"Careful." Jackson's secure clasp around her shoulders steadied her when she stumbled. Without his support, she'd have fallen many times on the trail. Slick leaves hid the rocks and roots.

"Keep putting one foot, or paw, in front of the other," he encouraged.

The herculean battle with Lilith had drained Morgan beyond anything she'd ever experienced during a grueling day of warrior training, or anything else, and unleashed the ice queen. Gaining control over her inner wolf by herself wasn't gonna happen. Help lay with the potentially lethal elixir in Jackson's pouch, and only Miriam could administer it. Sheer will power and his constant vigilance were all that kept her going forward.

If not for her wolf vision, she'd never detect the dim path snaking through the smudge of bending trees. Even that wasn't enough. Again, she lurched forward, almost toppled by her insidious skirts.

Jackson righted her. "You're OK."

She was tempted to tear off the colonial garb driving her mad, and drop down on all fours. Instinctively, she knew if the wolf took her over there'd be no coming back. She'd bound off into the wind-swept forest, attacking Lord only knows what or who. Unless her bond with Jackson proved stronger.

"Don't give in, Morgan, stay with me," he pleaded, his voice gruff with emotion. He spoke as if he knew her inner struggles. "You're in my pack, and my future mate. My soul mate. I never said it out loud before, but I'm telling you now."

And he was hers, if she could speak. And follow the conversation. She drifted between her mind and the ice queen's.

He brushed a kiss to her now furry cheek. "Everything'll work out. You'll see."

*Lord willing and the crick don't rise.* The country saying Uncle Don used to quote before he disappeared for parts unknown ran through her jumbled thoughts.

Well, the creek was swollen with rain and the wind beckoned almost irresistibly. A thin howl trailed in the distance, sounding a primal cry. *The call of the wild.*

*Who's that?* Her ears pricked beneath the cap and hood. There was something familiar about that howl. *Friend or foe?* Were they calling to her? She wanted to discover.

Jackson restrained her as he might a horse chomping at the bit. "No, Morgan. We're not investigating this now."

"That wasn't Wapicoli," Hawthorne said from behind them, his tread so silent it was undetectable.

"Nope." Jackson kept a tight hold on her. "Whoever it is must wait. We've got to get Morgan back. She's losing it."

*Where*? *What*? Thinking was difficult.

"Keep it together a little longer, Morgan," Jimmy urged, his footsteps almost as quiet as a cat's.

The kid was family, that much she knew, but exactly what he expected from her, she wasn't sure. Scents carried on the bracing night air. She sniffed the moist earth and fallen leaves, mingled with the unique signature of each woodland creature. The woods summoned her, ancient hunting grounds, with rocky outcroppings for dens. The domain of the wolf.

"We're heading home. To the lodge." Jackson continually drew her back.

Yes. She remembered now. *The lodge*. After a short time, it had become home. She was floating in and out of a foggy realm, with Jackson providing bearings.

He turned his head to scout each side of the trail. "Keep a sharp lookout behind you, Hawth. I don't want him leaping on us before we have a clue."

"Gotcha. Didn't think enemy werewolves were this close."

"I didn't know you had enemy werewolves." That Dilly girl with Hawthorne revealed her ignorance.

Jackson propelled Morgan forward. "We heard they're moving into Wapicoli territory. This may be a scout."

Dilly's footfall was easily detected. "Maybe it's just a regular wolf?" She sounded frightened.

"There are no regular wolves left in these mountains." Jackson shook his head, likely at the depth of her naiveté.

The high thin wail rose again. Nearer this time. Morgan could swear she knew that voice, though not how, but her pack must come first. This was inherent in her.

A growl rumbled in Jackson's throat. "Usurper. When Morgan's better, we'll track him down. Another wolf pack is all we need on top of the Panteras and Dilly's crazy mother."

"Maybe we can get them all to fight each other for us," Jimmy suggested.

"Excellent idea, Jimbo. The enemy of my enemy is my friend. Sort of. Keep your eyes peeled, ears open, and knives ready." Jackson drew his blade with one hand, while supporting Morgan with the other.

She didn't have a knife and couldn't wield the weaponized scarf. Praying she'd have no more to deal with this evening, she helped keep watch as best she could in her failing state. The present challenge demanded her all. And she was so hungry. The handful of jelly beans from the stash Jimmy shared with the group earlier hadn't lasted long. Rumbling stomachs were audible, and not only hers.

Jimmy waved at the trees. "He'll follow the sound of our bellies."

"I should have hunted us up some rabbits back when I first suggested it," Hawthorne reminded them. "But nobody wanted to stop and make a fire. Or eat them raw."

Morgan would now.

"Next time, we're packing *Scooby Snacks*," Jimmy

said.

Hawthorne snorted. "Woof. Woof. They're for dogs, Cubbie."

Jimmy didn't hesitate. "At this point, I think we'd all eat them."

No one disagreed with the kid. Morgan would snap them up by the boxful. They should've packed extra food for this excruciating outing, but they'd been in such a tearing hurry, and Miriam busy sewing the pocket inside her cloak.

Jackson aimed his knife at the lights flickering through the trees up ahead of them. "The lodge is only a little farther, Morgan. Keep going."

'A little farther' could mean two miles yet, she'd learned.

Dilly sucked in her breath. "Oh my. Lights through trees might be haints."

"What's that?" Jimmy posed the question for him and Morgan both.

"Haints are there, but ain't." Dilly's voice wavered. "Ghostlike."

*Hells bells.* Now they had *haints*?

Jimmy clucked at her. "Jeeze, Dilly. Thanks for cheering the troops."

"It's actually kind of scary, Jimmy." His sarcasm was lost on her. "Or the lights might be jack m'lanterns."

"*M'lanterns*, not O'lanterns?" Jimmy double-checked.

"Course. Jack O'lanterns are just carved pumpkins. While m'lanterns—" Her shudder was audible.

"I'm almost afraid to ask," he began.

"Sneaky devil lights to lure you from the path."

"To your destruction?" he suggested.

"Uh huh." She dragged her feet.

Jackson made an impatient sound. "Or, it might be the *lodge*. Come on, Dilly. Bad enough being out here with a werewolf on the prowl."

"But y'all are werewolves."

"You can't argue with that." Hawthorne muffled the mirth in his observation.

Morgan expected he'd do a lot of that if Dilly stuck around. She had no amusement to spare in her exhaustion, though. If not for Jackson's support, she'd be belly crawling.

Jimmy must be practically dead on his feet, too. Even so, he'd rather go on an adventure and return cursed, than attend school. Unless it was *Hogwarts*, he'd stipulated. The kid was what you called a trooper.

She qualified as a whiner, or would, if she could talk. By the time they reached the lodge, it seemed like a mirage. She was on the verge of total collapse, and Jackson carried her into the yard. Chilled to the marrow, she was ravenous enough to eat her companions, if she had the strength.

"Halleluiah! We made it without any attacks from haints." Hawthorne whirled Dilly around.

How he had the energy left for anything beyond sucking soup through a straw was beyond Morgan, and the silly girl actually giggled.

"They don't attack so much as spook you," Dilly clarified.

"Glad we avoided that too. And the wily jack m'lanterns." He tossed his hat in the air and caught it. "Let's eat."

The meaty scent mingling with wood smoke from

the kitchen hearth promised vital sustenance. Unless Miriam served Morgan's supper in a bowl for her to lap while lying on the floor, she'd never manage. She was all paws now, and utensils beyond her. *Whatever.* She'd devour it anyway, anyhow.

Everyone was eager to get out of the wind and chow down a hearty supper. Until a shadowy figure barred their way to the entrance.

*Okema.*

Chapter Seven
There's Something About Dilly

*Ding. Dang. Dong.* A warning tolled inside Morgan. How long had Okema prowled the yard waiting for them? More importantly, on a scale of one to a zillion, just how ballistic was he?

She hadn't expected to encounter his stern presence first thing on their return. Maybe she should have, considering they'd brought Dilly along. *Duh.*

*Oh, man.* Morgan was in no state for a sharp rebuke—or worse. What if he lit into the ditzy girl? Would they have to defend her?

*Good luck with that.* Morgan could scarcely stand and sagged in Jackson's arms. Tension tightened her spine, coiling in her empty belly.

Doubtless, the others shared her apprehension, with the possible exception of Jimmy. His superpower lay in keeping his cool and tapping into his brilliant mind.

Not Morgan. Any superpowers she had were confined to the wolf fast taking her over. Unless, she'd missed something.

Okema pivoted and stalked across the remainder of the yard and up the steps to the lodge. He opened the door and took a stance in the threshold facing them. Like a last stand.

*Holy freaking moly.* If it came to a showdown between him and their beleaguered band, he'd win. He wasn't the supreme alpha for nothing.

He beckoned them forward with the curl of his fingers.

"Come on." Apparently, Jackson had resigned himself to his fate. He braved the way out in front, carrying Morgan, her flapping cloak trailing over them both.

The mud-spattered group followed closely behind the pack leader, their apprehension thick in the air. Okema's intimidating presence had that effect on people and 'Were beings', which Morgan most certainly ranked among. You didn't get much more 'were' than this.

Hawthorne and Dilly pressed nearer to Jackson for security, both moral and physical. Jimmy simply looked on. She'd bet the kid's *Spidey-sense* tingled, though. Nobody was totally unfazed by Okema. Not even batboy.

Okema held up his hand, halting them at the base of the steps. "Stay. We will speak."

*Great.* The unfathomable chief might have to communicate with Morgan telepathically, if she lost consciousness. He'd done so in the past. Meanwhile, the mouthwatering aroma of meat roasting in the kitchen tormented her.

As before, on those rare occasions when she'd been in the presence of the secretive warrior, he stood straight and tall. Snowy hair flowed down over his buckskin coat to his waist, and three golden feathers fluttered from the two white braids knotted together at the top of his head. Buckskin moccasins reached halfway up long legs encased in leather pants. Despite his age of two hundred and eighty-five, he exuded energy. The man could recharge batteries.

It crossed her mind that she'd never observed Okema with a weapon—and just as quickly—that he didn't need one.

While the elusive chief was always around, somewhere, watching over the clan, he seldom joined the family for anything. She could count on her fingers the number of times she'd seen him since her arrival at the lodge, with fingers to spare. An occasional meal or gathering, usually to council her, comprised his visits. His presence here now was highly significant.

She could point this out to the others, if speech were possible, but doubted she needed to. They seemed duly mindful, even rattled.

Could they discern the bluish-white aura outlining Okema? Not all shared Morgan's recently acquired knack for detecting auras. At least, his wasn't fiery-red.

The orange glow from inside the massive stone and timber structure illuminated his lined face. His singular eyes glinted in the light of candles on stands in the entryway crafted from sections of tree trunks. The expression in their silvery depths was less than friendly.

*Crap.* They were in trouble.

He skimmed his tight gaze over the assembly and settled on Morgan. Those eyes pierced her soul, along with the sinking sensation that she'd failed him.

"Your mission was successful?" He addressed Jackson, as if knowing she couldn't speak.

*Heckfire.* Of course, he did. This mystical chief knew most everything. The questions must be a test.

A sigh heaved in Jackson's chest. "We've obtained the elixir for Morgan, but Jimmy got zapped in the process. We tried to make Lilith undo the spell, but—"

Again, Okema held up his hand. Lips pressed together in a thin line, he surveyed Jimmy, then wrinkled his nose as if at the stench of rotten fish. He must've gauged the damage done to the boy.

"Like poison, that woman." He parted his clamped jaws. "Yet she dares to speak ill of me. I never cursed a child."

Turning his sites on Dilly, he stared at her, or through her. "What have you to say for yourself, daughter of Lilith?"

If he'd referred to her as Satan's spawn, he couldn't have been more damning.

Morgan detected Dilly's racing heart, and she emitted the fear scent of a snared rabbit, but she didn't totally freak out. To give the girl credit, she faced Okema shakily. Strong men and 'weres' had quaked to do the same. Jackson had regaled Morgan with tales of those who'd fled Okema's wrath—or tried.

A silent Hawthorne at her side, Dilly lifted her quivery chin. "I'm real sorry about Mama, sir," she piped in an abnormally shrill tone.

"Okema," he corrected in his low, near growl.

"Yes, Okema sir." She waved trembling fingers at Morgan. "Mama didn't enchantify this one. She came like that wanting help." Dilly stopped and really looked at Morgan. "Holy cow, she's gotten worse. Anyway, I'm powerful sorry Mama spelled the boy. Sometimes she can be—" Her voice caught.

"A demon lizard," Okema pronounced.

Dilly gulped. "I was gonna say a pain to live with."

"Yet, she is also what I say." Okema didn't bend.

In a breathless swell, Dilly surged ahead. "I didn't know the lizard part, but she spells folks and puts some kind of enchantment on the shine. I thought she was only using gypsy charms, but now I think she might be a witch," Dilly confided in a hushed tone, as if imparting new info. "That's why I want to stay with you all. If you'll let me. I'm a good cook and can help out with the chores. Please, Okema sir. Don't send me back. My sister, Eve, hardly ever gets in trouble, but I always seem to. Mama can be real spiteful. She'll shut me up in my room or the woodshed. Only—" Dilly brightened for a moment. "I've gotten really good at disappearing."

Morgan feared Okema would snap at her for blathering. Instead, he weighed each word pouring from her mouth. "How do you disappear?"

"Well." Gesturing with her hands, Dilly launched into an explanation. "I think real hard on where I want to be. Not too far, mind. I'm not that good yet. But somewhere else, and then—wham. I'm there. It's a real cool trick."

He eyed her intently. "Show me. Where do you want to be?"

She pointed at the lodge. "Inside."

"Go then," he invited. "If you can get there without stepping past me."

Maybe she was super-fast? Morgan half expected a blur streaking ahead of them. But Dilly didn't race up the steps and duck around Okema.

One moment she was standing beside Hawthorne, and the next, she wasn't. With a big smile, she stuck her head out from behind Okema. "I'm here!"

Morgan joined everyone else staring at her.

"Yikes-a-rooney." Jimmy's exclamation pretty much summed up the general amazement.

71

"Pretty awesome. Huh?" Dilly preened.

Okema swiveled toward her. "Do you know other *tricks*?"

"No. I just learned this one. But I might learn others."

"Indeed. Use your gift wisely." He laid his hand on her shoulder above the parka and mass of red hair. "If you are loyal to the Wapicoli and helpful to the women you may remain with us."

A smile curved Dilly's lips and she beamed at him. "Thanks a bunch. You won't regret it."

The arch in his furrowed brow indicated he already did. "Hawthorne, guide our guest to the kitchen. Your mother kept the food warm for your return."

Eyes dazed, as though he'd landed on an alien planet inhabited by lizard people, Hawthorne skirted around Jackson and Morgan. "She's a freakin' witch," he muttered in passing.

"Heck yeah," Jackson said under his breath. "Wonder what she'll do next?"

"I thought it was neat," Jimmy contributed to the murmured exchange.

Hawthorne stepped tentatively into the lodge. Dilly claimed his arm like rightful prey. The plea for help he cast over his shoulder as she bore him away was pitiful. Did he fear she'd accidentally hex him?

Probably.

Okema motioned to Jimmy. "You, too. Go on and eat."

He didn't have to summon the kid twice. Jimmy took the steps two at a time and paused by Okema. He tilted his reddened face, encircled by the snug hood, at the chief. "Don't worry. I'm gonna train that thunderbird and fly it back to Lilith's. It'll peck her eyes out. She won't spell anybody ever again."

"*Gitche.* Good." Okema nodded his approval without any accompanying surprise. Miriam must've told him about the incubating egg, or he already knew.

Morgan suspected the latter.

"It's a done deal," Jimmy assured him.

Not quite, but Okema didn't harsh his mellow. The kid darted toward his long-awaited supper with a happy cry. Food fixed anything. Even curses. Especially if there were treats.

The aged fingers motioned to Jackson and Morgan. He mounted the steps with her slumped in his hold. She was growing giddy.

Okema laid his hand on her forehead. The current flowing through his palm into Morgan gave her a badly needed lift. "Miriam must tend to her at once. I had hoped Morgan would find the strength to overcome this. But she is more severely affected than I knew."

*Crapola.* That really was bad.

Jackson sidled from boot to boot with her in his grasp. "I'll take her to Grandma right away. Before I go, about Dilly. She insisted on coming with us. I didn't want to bring her. And I had no idea she was that powerful."

"Nor has she. You acted rightly. Better the girl is with us than against us," Okema emphasized. "If Lilith knew her power she would never let her come."

Revelation gleamed in Jackson's dark eyes. "I hadn't considered that." His gaze narrowed again. "What about the curse on Jimmy? Will you undo it?"

Okema regarded his grandson, six generations removed, for a long moment before he answered. "You and Morgan must undertake this task when she is better, with help from the others. I will not always be here to act in your stead. This will be your greatest challenge yet."

Jackson held his breath before speaking. Morgan could tell. "What if we fail?"

The stern gaze slid between them. "You will not fail. You will find a way. *You must*. The boy's life hangs in the balance. And more."

*What else?*

*You shall see, Wolf Girl*, Okema said in her head. *The fate of all depends on you.* He waved Jackson on. "Now go."

Chapter Eight
Potions and Plots

*Holy crap*. Could Morgan possibly get any less cool? If she hadn't resembled the wolf disguised as *Little Red Riding Hood's* grandma before, she sure as heck did now. She'd win a prize for best costume if this were Halloween, and the geeks didn't snag first place. Good thing it wasn't the big eve yet.

Wearing one of Miriam's long flannel nightgowns to accommodate her tail, she curled in bed under a pile of blankets. Even with the fire crackling in the hearth, casting shadows on the walls, she couldn't get warm. Hours out in the wet cold must've frozen her to the marrow. She'd even left the old-fashioned white cap tucked over her pointy ears. Still, she shook beneath the covers.

Miriam pulled a quilt up to Morgan's furry chin and adjusted the pillow under her head. "Chills and giddiness are the deteriorating effects from *Wandering Wolf*. Your body is trying to fight it off, like an infection. With the elixir, you will soon revive, and I added some willow bark to the brew to ease your fever."

*Lordy*, Morgan prayed the stuff worked. It tasted nasty enough, if that counted. She figured there was only one way to go when she'd sunk this low, and that was up. Unless she managed to claw herself a deeper hole.

Miriam sat on the bed beside her, lengths of silver hair spilling over the blue wool shawl draped around her shoulders. "Are you still hungry? I could bring you more stew."

Morgan shook her head. The three hearty bowlfuls she'd scarfed were the best food ever, she'd been so starved. No amount of honey added to the elixir, though, could fool her taste buds into thinking the bitter brew was manna from heaven.

At least, the stuff hadn't killed her. The potentially lethal poison was too risky for a less skillful herbalist to safely dispense. Thank heavens for Miriam.

"You're wondering how long it will take the potion to work its magic. Aren't you?" She posed the foremost question in Morgan's mind. "You should be improved by morning, but it may be several days before the remedy fully takes effect. Lilith supplied us with a generous portion of the herbs we needed, blended in the proper proportions." Miriam frowned. "A shame she couldn't let it go at that, and had to spell Jimmy."

*The understatement of the year. Well, one of them.*

Dark brown eyes, so like Jackson's, brimmed with determination. "You and my grandson will make this right. I have faith. As does Okema."

Oh, Morgan knew. And that wasn't all he expected from her, apparently.

Miriam laid a gentle hand on her furry brow. "Also, I should tell you that Dilly is sleeping on a cot in my room, instead of in here with you. We thought it best—" She hesitated. "Under the circumstances."

Did they arrive at this arrangement because Morgan had too much wolf in her to be entrusted with

Dilly's safety, or was Dilly too 'witchified' to roam beyond Miriam's sight? She was definitely a loose cannon, and Morgan not exactly stable.

Even a tiny improvement in her condition would be gleefully welcomed. The woodsy spice of cedar emanating from the pervasive use of the wood in every single piece of furniture in this room filled her still wolfish nose. The pleasing fragrance, reminiscent of a freshly cut Christmas tree, was supposed to have a calming effect.

*Nope.* She required more than this to soothe the troubled beast. And didn't need the magic *Mirror Mirror on the wall* to see her wolf self, as Miriam had allowed her to first glimpse the ice queen, using a spell. Heaven only knew what else the woman was capable of, and it boggled the mind to contemplate the full capacity of Okema.

Had the prophetic chief actually said *the fate of all* depended on Morgan? Did he mean *all the Wapicoli*, or the whole freaking world? The fate of the clan was enough responsibility to lay at her door, without making the threat global.

What about Jackson? He was in on the savior thing too, she assumed. He'd better be. His destiny was equally as important as Morgan's, according to the prophecy from the Star People. The space aliens had imparted their wisdom and 'gifts' to Okema, if having the spirit of a wolf and seven lifetimes constituted such. In addition to that knowledge, he was blessed with insights which he shared in maddening snippets.

Why had he spoken in Morgan's head so only she heard? He'd said they faced their greatest challenge yet, then added that final zinger for her benefit. Well, no kidding! She'd enlighten Jackson as soon as full speech returned.

Surely, Miriam didn't expect more from them than saving Jimmy? Wasn't that overwhelming enough without piling on more? Gazing at the insightful woman, she willed her to answer.

Miriam observed Morgan as if she saw her thoughts whirring, each one resonating within her. "Yes. Jackson told me what Lilith wants. Though what her end purpose is, I have not yet fathomed. Nor do I trust it. Still..." She spoke softly, sliding her fingers over Morgan's forehead in slow circles. "In order to obtain the serpent's fang you must first make contact with Santiago. Not easily done."

The woman was full of understatements tonight.

"And convince him to hand over the fang on the silver necklace around his neck," she forged ahead. "This seems impossible, doesn't it?"

*You think?* Santiago probably inherited the toothy heirloom and cherished it above all other worldly possessions.

"Remember Okema telling you the Panteras were originally Spanish pirates, in addition to being panther shifters?" Wood popped in the hearth, sending up a shower of sparks, and dancing shadows lent eeriness to Miriam's whispers.

Morgan nodded. She wasn't so delirious she'd forgotten that bizarre account.

"And they wrecked along the Virginia coast after being chased by the Royal Navy, and came inland to the mountains to hide their treasure?" Miriam prompted.

A short nod. Morgan was with her so far.

"After the bulk of the pirates grew restless and left, taking as much plunder with them as they could carry, the remainder was guarded by the one who stayed behind. Santiago descends from him and bears his name."

Another spray of sparks seemed to confirm Miriam's disclosure, one Morgan recalled. Was it purely her imagination, or did the flames take the form of an orange panther?

Firelight flickering behind her, Miriam bent toward Morgan. "Then you also know Mateo, leader of the city Panteras, wants the treasure back?"

*Oh, yes.* An accompanying chill shivered through Morgan at the reminder.

A conspiratorial glint lit Miriam's eyes. "If you struck a deal with Santiago to fight with the Mountain Panteras against Mateo and his city gang, maybe he'd be more obliging about the serpent's fang."

Morgan drew back. Had Miriam gone nuts?

"I know you think I'm crazy," she began.

*No, duh.*

"But consider this." She closed her fingers around Morgan's shoulder. "True, the Mountain Panteras are our enemy, but not on the scale inflicted by Mateo and his gang. And *both* are warring with each other. A truce with Santiago, even a temporary one, and uniting our forces to fight Mateo, might hold sway. And not be a bad thing, in the end."

*The end of them all*, Morgan would bet.

"Have you a better idea?" Miriam inquired, knowing full well Morgan hadn't.

Without the benefit of a voice, she couldn't insist she did. The fact was, she didn't have a clue, and

Miriam was wise. Usually, anyway.

"I only ask that you ponder my suggestion, one I shall also make to Jackson. You cannot possibly hope to sneak the necklace off Santiago's neck without him noticing. Not even with the aid of Dilly, who can teleport, I'm told." Miriam snorted at this.

*Doggone.* So, that's what her disappearing act was called.

The creases in Miriam's brow deepened. "We're keeping a sharp eye on that one, I can tell you."

As soon as Morgan was back on her feet, not paws, she'd do the same. And confer, cuddle, and canoodle with Jackson. She wasn't actually sure what canoodle meant, but it sounded good flowing through her fevered mind.

Her companion pressed a kiss to her forehead, then rose in a rustle of skirts. "Enough scheming for now. Rest, dear girl. You shall need all your strength for what lies ahead. I will check on you again soon." She glided to the door, pausing with her hand on the knob. "When you are better I will give you the letter from Sarah Morgan. Perhaps you will find insight in her words."

Perhaps so. Grandma Sarah had ministered to Morgan before in a phenomenal way. She'd worn her clothes all day. They had an uncanny bond between them. Sarah's voice reaching from the past might help now.

Chapter Nine
Voice from the Past

Wandering Wolf had hit Morgan hard. After two long days of tossing and turning in bed, she could finally sit up, propped against pillows, without lightheadedness assaulting her. Since their return from Lilith's, she hadn't stirred from her room. Huddled under her blankets, she'd drifted in and out of consciousness, dreaming weird dreams.

Witches, Panteras, slimy swamp creatures, and werewolves floated through her tormented sleep. One particularly menacing werewolf was oddly familiar. If any meaning could be drawn from these ghoulish visitations, though, Morgan couldn't discern what that might be. Much as she tried.

"Do not distress yourself. It's simply the fever talking," Miriam assured her, finding Morgan's temperature more difficult to lower than she'd expected, even with her arsenal of herbs.

The dedicated healer didn't give up for a moment. She battled on, appearing in Morgan's bedroom regularly with doses of the elixir and other concoctions. Nourishing meals wafting pleasing aromas, and hot tea with milk and sugar, arrived in a timely fashion. Feeding Morgan also played a big role in Miriam's treatment plan. Along with the food and medicines, she bore messages from Jackson and everyone else she'd banned from seeing Morgan. She'd even aided her in going to and from the bathroom. Embarrassing to have sunk this low.

"Weak as water," Miriam had proclaimed her. Getting better, she'd insisted, was Morgan's top priority, which meant rest, and more rest.

Miriam brooked no argument, and Morgan had been too feeble to resist. No longer. At last, the promise of returning strength fluttered within her, tingling in her veins. She was ready to open the letter waiting in the dusty trunk all these years—for her.

"I shall leave you to it and check back later." Miriam thoughtfully allowed Morgan some privacy and left the room.

Flickering candlelight, exuding the sweetness of beeswax, played over the yellow parchment she held in her now human hand. Beyond this, the glow from the fireplace illuminated the ancient paper. With a sense of disbelief, Morgan broke the red wax seal and unfolded the creased page.

She scanned the carefully penned script. No one bothered with the graceful curls and arches in their letters these days, unless they were skilled calligraphers. Then the alphabet became a work of art. Hardly able to believe this message was actually from her colonial grandmother, she read.

*Dearest daughter of my daughters,*

*I have foreseen your name shall be Morgan and I am glad. Though I was forced to leave the family and dwell apart from them in secret, Daniel Morgan will ever be my adored father. My retreat into exile was necessary for their protection. I believe you understand why that is, and share my struggles.*

Oh, yes. Morgan empathized keenly. After her supernatural encounter with Grandma Sarah on the night of the full moon, when she'd faded into the spirit world, she'd heard her soft voice. She almost heard her now, speaking in her ear.

*My dear girl. As I dip my quill in the ink and ponder what to impart, I consider how strange it must seem to you to receive a missive composed more than two hundred years ago. I assure you, Morgan, you are near in my thoughts, though the hour of your birth lies far in the hazy distance. I wonder how I might explain myself so you will better understand.*

Morgan didn't lift her eyes from the page. Images flooded her mind of Grandma Sarah seated at an eighteenth century desk, bent to the task. The very clothes she'd worn then might be folded in the trunk. Perhaps they were the ones Morgan had journeyed in. Either way, the realization gave her goosebumps. She'd met the young Sarah in her dreamy state that night, like gazing into a mirror. The resemblance between them left no doubt she was Morgan's ancestor. Awe coursed through her.

*Some say I am a prophetess to glimpse the future as I do. They proclaim my sight a gift. Others hurl charges of witchcraft at my feet and threaten me with the flames. I tell you truly, I am neither angel nor demon. I am Sarah, the one who sees, and walks as a wolf when the moon calls. Few know my dark secret, as few may know yours. Yet none dare to lay a hand on me. They fear to perish, and rightly so. I will not suffer their abuse. Nor should you. Thus, I am left to my visions, my healing herbs, and silent thoughts.*

Good heavens. Morgan envisioned the female

figure shrouded in the green cloak she'd worn, walking the murky woods alone, with threats of a fiery death hanging over her. Did they still burn witches back then? What of werewolves?

She shuddered, grateful Sarah had been willing and able to defend herself. So was Morgan, thanks to this determined woman. She read on.

*Alas, my beloved husband is no longer with me. My daughter, Grace, is my joy. Through Grace, shall come other daughters, until the years fall away likes leaves in the autumn and your blessed birth occurs. Dear child, your time is yet to be, while mine draws to an end. As my days dwindle like the last grains of sand sifting through an hour glass, I carry you in my prayers, and lift my voice to heaven. Surely, a petition as pure as mine must be heard by the Almighty?*

*For you, Morgan, the Seventh One to come after me, I pray happiness and love may find you in all fullness. I foresee your calling and the weight you must bear. If the saints allow, I will watch over you. Look for me by moonlight, seek me in the dusk, hear me in the wind, I am there.*

Shivers darted through Morgan, and not from fever. She knew now. Sarah had always been with her, and would continue to be. She savored the last passage of the letter.

*What advice can I give you? Only this. Do not be ruled by anger. Yes, you were cursed, as was I, yet also gifted by the moon. Listen to the deepest recesses of your innermost self. Heed the wisdom it imparts, and that of those who have earned your trust. May you find the strength to fulfill your quest, and may God keep you safely in his care.*

*Your loving grandmother from the mists of time,*
*Sarah Daniel, the first Morcant*

How long—minutes, hours—Morgan clutched the parchment to her chest, she couldn't say. Those words had captured her imagination and her heart. The kindling in the fireplace popped and crackled, and the candles burnt low, as she sat, lost in thought.

Miriam discovered her like this on her return with the evening dose of medicine steaming in a teacup. Mingled herbs scented the air with mint, spice, a touch of apple, and the usual aromatic pungency, as they regarded each other. No words were needed between them. Miriam seemed to possess an innate understanding of what the letter had meant to Morgan, if her expression and the way she clasped the parchment wasn't a giveaway.

Remembering Sarah's advice to heed the wisdom of those she trusted, Morgan resolved to follow Miriam's. She refolded the letter, laid it on the bedside stand made from the polished section of a tree trunk, and reached for the cup. She knocked back the potent brew with barely a grimace.

"I will speak to Jackson about carrying out your scheme with Santiago," she promised. "You have my word."

"*Megwich*. Thank you. I think that's best." Miriam's voice was nearly as soft as Sarah's had been. "Be forewarned, he'll take some convincing."

Morgan could well imagine. "I'm not surprised he balked, but will do my best to persuade him."

A watery smile lit Miriam's gaze. "Your best is better than mine, no doubt. You are mending just in time, too. Tomorrow is Halloween and the big party at the lodge."

This news gave Morgan a jolt. She'd forgotten the day. "Oh, right. You've all been busily scurrying around while I'm lying here in slug mode."

Miriam took the empty cup she extended. "Not your fault you've been down. Besides, the boys are excited and don't mind helping out. Even Jackson's taken an interest this year. He wants the party to be extra special for you, and was terribly worried you wouldn't be well enough to attend."

Warmth welled in Morgan, along with anticipation. "How sweet. Tell him I'll be there with bells on. And I know exactly who I'm going as."

"Sarah Morgan," Miriam surmised.

"Actually, she'd changed her last name to Daniel by the time of this letter. But yes, I'm eager to see what else I might find in that trunk. A gown possibly…"

Visions of herself royally dolled up, after days as a bedraggled half-wolf, appealed to Morgan. She wanted to wow Jackson and dance—

The firm look from Miriam checked her enthusiasm. "That discovery can wait until the morning. A good night's sleep will top you off. I added a generous dollop of valerian and chamomile to the brew. You will soon be sunk among those pillows, dozing peacefully. And I shall watch that you are."

A bittersweet chord resounded in Morgan. "You remind me of her, of Sarah." Despite the distinct differences between the two women.

Miriam's eyes glistened. "Kindred spirits can connect across the boundaries of race, even of time and space. I care for you like my own granddaughter."

"Yes." The quaver in Morgan's voice stemmed

from high emotion. Normally, she wasn't much of a hugger—with the exception of Jackson, whom she'd gladly embrace anytime—but she owed Miriam a great debt.

Reaching out both arms, she wrapped them around Miriam's slender figure and embraced her as if she really meant it, because she did. "Without you, I'd have succumbed to my affliction."

"Dear child." Miriam held her close, then drew back and smoothed strands of hair from her damp face. "You will learn to be one with the wolf. Not in battle with her, or in dominion over her, or she over you, but working together as two halves of the same whole. This is essential. This is the key. You shall see."

Like rays of purest light, the truth of Miriam's quiet assertion reached deep inside Morgan and she believed. One major hurdle was won. Many challenges loomed ahead, like craggy mountains of sheer rock to scale. She mustn't focus on that. For now, this was a huge victory.

Chapter Ten
The Belle of the Ball

What had Morgan done now? She must've been out of her freakin' skull to turn Dilly loose on her hair and makeup in preparation for the big eve. Wafting the potent 'Take me now' musk Dilly had misted her with, she sat rigidly on the chair in her bedroom, white knuckling the wooden arms.

Had it been an hour? Two? Time crawled while Dilly separated each section of her hair with the pointy end of a comb and used the curling iron mercilessly. She'd fry every strand, and Morgan had a lot of hair.

Wapicoli Lodge possessed a generator for limited electricity, although candles and hearths were favored, and burned in the bedroom now. Dilly located an outlet for her wand, and laid the tools of her trade on the rustic stand. An odd blend of old and new.

Multiple clips found their way into Dilly's evolving creation. If these weren't adequate to hold the elaborate 'do' in place, the amount of spray she'd used could withstand a gale force wind. Then she started on Morgan's face.

*Lord have mercy.* The zealous girl was applying enough makeup for three women.

*Crap, not false eyelashes, too.* "Seriously, Dilly. I don't think we need—"

She brushed aside Morgan's protest. "You want to

slay Jackson, don't you?"

He wouldn't know her from *Effie Trinket* of *Hunger Games* fame, at this rate.

On went the lashes, with Morgan blinking and Dilly insisting she 'hold still' until they were cemented in place. She'd probably have them for life.

If she swore, she surely would now. "Dilly, I'm hungry. And tired, and—"

"Whiner." Her attendant popped a peppermint in Morgan's mouth. "They'll have plenty to eat at the party. Now, sit!"

Sucking the mint, Morgan did as Dilly bid, but the *ooohs*, *ahhhs*, and *awesomes* in her running commentary, with no accompanying visual, had her ready to crack. Maybe it was just as well she couldn't view Dilly's endeavors. The possessed *artiste* wanted to *surprise* her at the end with a great reveal.

Would a dead faint be an adequate indication of her astonishment?

Dilly spritzed on more sparkle, because, heaven knew, Morgan didn't have enough already.

Another blast of glitter descended over her like fallout.

*For cripes sake.* Surely, Dilly must be done by now.

"Nearly finished?" Morgan prompted, in what would've been dry mouthed apprehension, except for the moisture from the mint. "How do I look?"

Dilly paused with the compact she'd lightly pressed over Morgan's skin, to 'set the makeup'. "Drop-dead gorgeous."

"Really?" She perked up. Would normal people agree?

"Come and see." Dilly laid the compact in the case on the stand, and assisted Morgan to her feet. Not as easy to rise in billowing skirts as one might think. The hem brushed the floor as she ventured hesitantly to the mirror.

"Score!" Dilly flung up a triumphant hand dusted with sparkles. "Jackson won't recognize you."

*What the...? Who the...?* Morgan didn't recognize herself.

Shock parted her dusky rose lips, outlined in a deeper shade of rose. A touch of gloss was the most she'd ever added before. Not that Dilly had neglected the gloss; a layer glazed the lipstick. Dilly had used a sealant on that first, 'to hold the color', she'd said. These lips were never coming off.

To give the creator credit, Dilly had definitely achieved an effect beyond anything Morgan could've imagined. Ever. The look ranged somewhere between prom queen extraordinaire, a beauty pageant contestant, and *Cinderella*, although she doubted even the fairy godmother had gone this all out.

There were no words.

"Gobsmacked, are you?" Dilly prompted.

"Totally." She attempted to stammer the expected appreciation. "I—wow—just wow."

Morgan was spending the evening in her room.

The beaming girl hovered at her side, tucking stray curls in place, and admiring her handiwork. "I used the colors of the night sky for your makeup. Well, mostly. You *really* needed bronzer and that's more a daytime shade. Way cool, isn't it?"

"Uh huh." At least, Morgan wasn't Goth.

Deep twilight blue outlined her widened stare and

enhanced the color of her dazed eyes. The heavy lashes made keeping them open a challenge, but hey, she didn't want to appear ungrateful, and kept that observation to herself. Perhaps, they took getting used to. She hoped so, as they were likely permanent.

Dilly waved at her. "I dusted moonbeam white on your eyelids. Don't you love it?"

"Sure do." Undulating shades of plum spread above her lids to plucked and penciled brows—a painful procedure.

The bronzed blush highlighting her cheekbones and touching her chin, nose, and forehead gave her a sun kissed radiance. True, she did need extra color, with the pallor leftover from her recent illness. Now she resembled a sun worshiper who'd spent her days at the beach.

Could she possibly glisten anymore? It looked like an explosion at the pixie dust factory had covered her head and every available skin surface. Technically, with enough happy thoughts, she should be able to fly. "Even the diamond dusted vamps in *Twilight* can't out glitz me."

"Nope." Dilly curved crimson lips in a dazzling smile. "Vampires aren't real, you know? At least, not here."

"Yeah. Jackson told me." They were one of the few threats absent from these mountains.

Morgan couldn't take her eyes from her reflection, and not only because they were difficult to shift with the false lashes. Beyond the makeup disguising her, were she to seek a new identity, was the hair that grabbed her jaw-dropping attention. The blond lengths were coiled high on her head with curling tendrils falling down around her shoulders.

She held onto Dilly, not from affection so much as the need for support. "This is some hairdo, girlfriend."

"Awesome, isn't it?" Dilly pointed proudly at her trove of supplies. "And I had all the stuff in my backpack. Can you believe it? Of course, I crammed it full and it's a big pack."

"Amazing. Most girls don't travel with this many beauty products." Maybe Dilly shouldn't have.

Blue-green eyes outlined in black liner shone, and Dilly exuded the sweetness of success. "Be prepared, I always say. Besides, I've wanted to be a stylist since I was a kid, and set up shop at home." She sighed. "But nobody would come to the house with mama spelling them."

"That's a deal breaker, all right. Maybe you could work somewhere else?" Some place they wouldn't notice Dilly's witchified tendencies. "Not the lodge," she hastened to add.

An eye roll followed Morgan's reminder. "That buzzkill chief would never let me." A pout turned down the corners of Dilly's red mouth.

Foolish girl. She was fortunate Okema had allowed her to remain and not killed her on the spot when she'd first arrived, and added her to his collection buried out back. But Morgan didn't point this out. She didn't need Dilly waving those fingers about any more than she already did when she spoke. No sense in risking an accidental hex. God, alone, knew what else she'd inherited from her demonic mother.

"One more thing." Dilly darted to her backpack and returned with small bows in hand. She clipped them here and there in the mound of curls on Morgan's head.

Like the spritz, they also sparkled.

She'd swear she could double as a Christmas tree. "You really are inspired in your work."

Dilly pinkened with pleasure. "Yes, well. When you said you wanted to wear that fancy dress from way back when, I thought how they wore their hair real high in the olden days, with curls. This look is perfect for it."

Granted, Morgan recalled seeing portraits of ladies from earlier centuries with high flung, even bizarre, hairstyles. She expected Grandma Sarah's had been far simpler. Oh well, it was Halloween. "I'd fit right into the past," she agreed. They had masquerades then, too.

"I know! Right?" Dilly nudged her. "Go on. Give the dress a twirl."

"Oh. OK." She might as well. Her hair wasn't going anywhere.

Lifting the skirts of her yellow-gold gown, the most formal one Morgan had discovered in the trunk, she spun around. The taffeta fabric swished as she turned, and the lace hanging from her fluted sleeves whirled. Lace also adorned her low neckline and the ruffles at her skirt. She'd been roped into the corset to fit into the gown, giving her actual cleavage, and she wore two petticoats beneath. Truly, she'd suffered greatly for beauty.

Dilly clapped her hands. "You must feel like a princess. You look straight out of a fairy tale."

Morgan stopped revolving. "I suppose I do." She definitely wasn't of this world.

"I've got it!" Dilly beamed. "You're Beauty and the Beast both. The Beast on wolf days, and Beauty in between. Especially now. Not that the wolf isn't pretty too," she amended.

"Right. Thanks." Morgan gave a final twirl, admiring the sheen of candlelight on the burnished cloth, and the glints of light in the moonstone around her neck. She turned to the would-be cosmetologist/hair dresser. "What are you going as?"

Dilly was outfitted in tight black leather pants and a form-fitting black sweater dusted with sparkle from making up Morgan, and black boots. Hawthorne might be kind of freaked out by Dilly's *gifts*, but he'd be wowed. They all would.

"A cat burglar?" Morgan suggested, given the tight fitting black.

Peals of laughter erupted at her suggestion. "Close. *Catwoman*, you know, from *Batman*?"

"Oh, right. I know all about superheroes and super villains. Jimmy's really into them. And Hawthorne."

Dilly glowed at the mention of his name. "I just have to draw on my whiskers with eyeliner, get the ears I made—they're attached to a headband—and I'm ready to party."

"Sure are. You'll look great."

"Thanks." Dilly was so happy Morgan didn't have the heart to remind her cats weren't highly favored among the Wapicoli, given that Panteras were their mortal enemies.

Maybe lethal relations would improve with Santiago and the Mountain Panteras, if the pact she and Jackson attempted was successful. They'd met with Miriam earlier today. Together, the women had persuaded him to give it a try. They hadn't had the opportunity yet to work out the details of the best way to go about making an initial contact. Tricky.

Soon, they would. For now, the big eve lay before

her, if she dared venture forth like this. Doors opened and closed downstairs, and animated voices carried from below. The night was getting underway.

What was she thinking? She couldn't possibly hurt Dilly's feelings, and she didn't want to miss out on the fun.

*Screw vanity.* Jackson had seen her as a half-dead wolf. This couldn't be any worse, maybe even better.

She turned to Dilly. "Want to go down together?"

"Be back in a minute." And like that, Dilly was gone.

The girl sure was taken with teleporting. Morgan ought to caution her not to overdo—

A rap on the bedroom door disrupted her conjecture. Lifting her skirts, she drifted across the room in a most ladylike manner, the only way to keep from tripping over her gown. She turned the knob and opened the door to find Jackson standing there in all his masculine glory, dressed like a dashing Westley from *The Princess Bride.*

He'd pulled his long hair back in a ponytail and wore a black mask over his eyes. A cape of the same midnight hue parted in front to reveal the matching long-sleeved shirt covering his broad chest, fashioned in the style of an earlier age. Lengths of the cape fell around his jet-black leather pants and boots. The sheathed sword suspended from the leather belt at his waist looked quite real, and probably was.

When had he taken up fencing? A lot had happened while she was down.

Admiration flooded her. "Magnificent," she breathed out.

It was difficult to tell with his mask, but his dark

brown eyes appeared to be riveted on her. "Morgan?"

She knew he wouldn't recognize her! "Who else? And don't say *Effie Trinket*."

"I wasn't." Before she uttered another syllable, he closed his arm around her middle and bent his head, covering her protesting mouth with his warm lips.

Heat rushed through her in a pounding current. *Finally*! Jackson hadn't kissed her in days. Not that she blamed him, considering the circumstances, but she'd begun to wonder if he even felt this way about her anymore. She was wild about him.

His scent also made her heady, a meld of the forest, wood smoke, and his own unique wolf musk. She hadn't realized that's what it was when they first met, but she knew now.

He held her closer, and deepened his kiss, leaving her in no doubt as to his feelings for her. She grew breathless.

Sliding his lips to her ear, he whispered. "I've missed you so much. Thank God you're OK. Better than OK. Terrific."

"Even with my hair and everything?"

He nuzzled her cheek. "It's a new look for you, but you're always gorgeous. Besides, I like the dress." He chuckled. "Especially what it *doesn't* cover."

"I'll bet. But the gown comes with the makeup and you'll be wearing my lipstick now," she warned, between shallow pants.

Showing her how little that concerned him, he covered her mouth again with his, and clutched her to his hard chest. She melted against him.

*No mating before marriage. No marriage before eighteen*, ran through her pulsing mind. Okema had been unyielding.

*Both* of them had to reach that age first, or something dire would transpire. He hadn't said what, only that they'd mess with the darn prophecy. Not done. The wait was gonna be doubly difficult and—

Dilly popped back in as suddenly as she'd exited. "Told ya you'd slay him!"

Morgan couldn't argue with that.

Whiskers penciled on and ears in place, Dilly explored Jackson appreciatively. "Who are you supposed to be?"

He released Morgan, stepped back, and drew his sword. "Guess," he invited, slashing his blade in the air and thrusting at an invisible opponent. "I swagger, fight, and laugh in the face of danger."

"Batman?" the clueless girl suggested.

Jackson whirled his cape. "Never heard of him. I'm a swashbuckler from a long, illustrious line of daring dudes."

"How cool is that?" Dilly gestured excitedly. "Have you buckled any swashes?"

"Heaps." Exchanging amused glances with Morgan, Jackson sheathed his sword, and extended a gentlemanly arm to each of them. "Ladies, shall we descend the stairs and join the festivities?"

"There's nothing I should prefer more, sir." Morgan took his arm. "Do you have an official title?"

"Sir will do. Don't want to give away my true identity," he smiled.

"You bear a striking resemblance to the *Man in Black*," she suggested.

"Yeah. I get that a lot. And Jimmy keeps muttering *inconceivable*." He shrugged in feigned bemusement.

Morgan muffled a snort. But his humor was lost on Dilly.

She took his other arm. "Do you know who I am?"

"Batgirl?" he teased.

She brightened. "No, but that's a good idea. Guess I should lose the cat ears, make bat ones, find a cape..." she mused aloud, lost in creative thought.

This could take a while if Dilly really got inspired. Morgan nodded toward the stairs. "Shall we head on down?"

Eyes dancing behind his mask, Jackson flicked her a wink. "As you wish."

Her heart drummed in her corset. Should she tell him his lips were streaked with rose, or let Hawthorne?

Chapter Eleven
All Hallows' Eve

*What a rush*! Halloween at the lodge was completely different from what Morgan had experienced in the past. No trick or treaters crowding the door. Zero worries about running out of candy and having to 'go dark' and hide in a blacked out room to avoid the eggers. No kids sneaking through the yard, TP-ing the shrubbery.

Most exhilarating of all, hands down, no contest, was Jackson at her side. Sort of like going to the prom together on a real date, the closest stellar event she could possibly compare this evening to. She'd never actually been to a prom, but grasped the concept. Moving from place to place, always on the run, had cramped her social life, such as it was.

"Wanna go to the prom?" some cute guy would text her, and *wham*! Aunt M. hustled them out the door and into another town practically before she hit *send*.

Roots were something plants had. Not Morgan. Maybe she had a shot at putting down roots in these mountains.

Besides, none of those would be boyfriends she'd missed out on dating were in the same sphere as Jackson. Not even the same planet. She had the boyfriend to top all boyfriends.

Lifting her skirts with her free hand to keep from

tripping over the hem and spoiling the delectable moment, she swished down the steps on his arm. Awe swelled inside and tingles shimmered to her toes in the gold high-heeled shoes Miriam had found for her. She hadn't asked how, or where. Maybe it was magic. The whole evening was magical.

Jackson made her feel elegant, despite Dilly overdoing her hair and makeup. The ability to walk gracefully in this floor-length gown took some mastering, and upped her appreciation of Grandma Sarah and other ladies from bygone eras. Men had no idea what a feat this was.

Nor did Dilly. Unencumbered by rustling skirts, she easily descended the steps on Jackson's other side. If the girl had any anxiety over immersing herself in the Wapicoli clan on this hallowed eve, she gave no indication. Perhaps, she ought to have a few reservations. After all, they were werewolves. Morgan supposed Dilly could always teleport, or zoom away on her broomstick, if need be. But she doubted a hasty departure would be necessary. Surely, everyone would be on their best behavior tonight.

"Oh, wow." Pausing partway down the steps, Morgan swept her gaze over the entryway.

Carved jack O'lanterns with glowing faces greeted her from atop rustic stands and luminous corners. Cornstalks bundled together stood like sentinels on either side of the front door. Colorful gourds, and bunches of Indian corn tied with twine, encircled the sheaths. A garland of preserved fall leaves dotted with orange-red bittersweet berries and glossy acorns hung above the doorway and trailed down over the sides. Normally, the stout barrier was bolted shut. Tonight, they'd left it unbarred to welcome costumed guests. This remote clan sure loved to dress up. She spotted superheroes, fairy tale characters, *Power Rangers*, even Elvis, in the mix of adults and children spilling into the hall.

*Holy Moly*! Miriam stood in the entryway welcoming people while dressed in the traditional tall black hat and long cape of a witch. She had a wand in her hand, and waved them on with it after her initial greeting.

Morgan nudged Jackson. "What about the Wapicoli not liking witches?" she whispered.

He gave her a wry smile. "Surreal. But it's Halloween. Grandma can be whoever she wants."

Actually, Morgan rather thought it suited her. She'd always suspected Miriam was some kind of witch; a good one.

"What a super hype party!" Dilly erupted from the other side of Jackson.

"Yeah," Morgan agreed. "Jimmy would probably say 'zounds!' Where is Batboy, anyway?"

"No-brainer." Jackson grinned. "I'm betting he's parked beside the refreshments with Hawth."

At Hawthorne's name, Dilly disappeared in the blink of an eye and reappeared ahead of them in the crowded hall.

"That's one way to get out in front," he said matter-of-factly. "I doubt she even realizes she's doing it anymore."

Morgan nodded. "It's becoming alarmingly second nature to her. Makes you wonder what's next?"

"Sure does. Come on, my lady. Plenty more to see." He escorted her down the remaining steps and into the throng.

Miriam glanced around at their coming. Her eyes widened upon spotting Morgan. She'd probably already viewed Jackson's costume, maybe even assisted him with it, but Morgan's transformation must be a bit of a shock. She needn't have worried, though. Miriam's lips curved in a smile. Nodding her approval, she waved the swashbuckler and his colonial style *Effie Trinket* girlfriend on with her wand.

Morgan arched on her tiptoes to speak in Jackson's ear. "Is that wand made of holly with the feather of a phoenix in its core, by any chance?"

He chuckled. "Like H.P.'s wand?"

"And *He-Who-Must-Not-Be-Named*, who has its twin."

"Quite possibly. I wouldn't put it past Grandma to cast a spell with it."

Neither would Morgan.

"Hey, man!" Jackson lifted his hand at a couple dressed as a cowboy and cowgirl with a small cow in tow.

Recognizing Roan Wapicoli, his red-headed wife, Annie, and shy son, Simeon, Morgan raised her hand. Eyebrows arched, but the couple smiled and returned the gesture. Simeon hugged his father's knees and buried his face.

"Hardly knew you, Morgan!" Roan called above the noise. He gave her a thumbs up. "Looking good!"

"*Megwich*! You guys, too!" Further conversation was nearly impossible, and anyone she'd met at the last bash wasn't recognizable now. If she remembered their names. Doubtful.

Jackson dropped his eyes to hers. "Got a surprise

for you."

"Good one?" It was difficult to determine his expression behind the mask.

"I'll let you be the judge of that." A definite lip twitch accompanied his reply.

Waving as he went, he steered her through the gathering, excited children chattering like birds, and hung a left into the large main room. She stopped beside him, staring at the Halloween wonderland spread before them—Wapicoli style.

Jack O'lanterns, their faces aglow, lined the log walls and grinned from every surface. Some orange beauties, large enough to transform into Cinderella's coach, were left uncarved. It took a lot of heave-ho to get them in here, but werewolves were strong.

Had they grown all the pumpkins themselves? Probably. These people were pumpkin mad. Made sense, though. This Halloween favorite came from the Native Americans.

White candles drew her interest to the refreshment table set up across the room in front of the seriously big bookshelves built against one wall. The candle holders were fashioned from lichen encrusted branches and antler prongs—all natural materials. Even the tiny tea lights floating in the glass punch bowl were made from the halves of walnut shells. Cookies and cupcakes decorated with pumpkins, ghosts, and black cats covered plates patterned with leaf designs. Popcorn balls wrapped in netting and tied with ribbon filled hollow, painted gourds. The Wapicoli were the Martha Stewart's of the forest.

More garlands of preserved fall leaves, bittersweet berries, and acorns draped the table, wound around the ceiling, and entwined the rafters. She craned her neck. The affronted owl must've taken cover and was nowhere in sight.

"Whewww," she whistled. "Somebody's been busy."

"Many hands make light work, or so I'm told." Jackson didn't sound entirely convinced. "Some of the women, including Aunt Willow, are in the kitchen fixing more treats. They've even roped my dad and Uncle Buck into helping."

"They really are going all out to do that. Worth it. Fab party." The brilliant decorations enriched an already vibrant room with its woven wall hangings and wood carvings of forest animals, wolves being the most prominent among them.

"Oh, look. There's Batboy." As predicted, Jimmy clanked around in his metal *Iron Man* costume near the refreshments. "Impressive getup."

"Yeah. I helped him weld that." Jackson singled out Hawthorne, in animated conversation with Dilly. "And I lent a hand with the *Wolverine* look. What do you think?"

"Sweet. Hawth's got the sideburns and funky hair thing going on—"

"With a lot of gel," Jackson added.

"Right. And the white muscle shirt doesn't look bad on him," she conceded, with an admiring glance. "But he's got to lose those hand blades if he wants to dance."

Jackson snorted. "With Dilly's curves, that's a yes."

"Figured." The warmup twang of guitars caught her ear. She swiveled her head at the band assembled at the far end of the room before the massive stone hearth.

The flames illuminated the four musicians, all male. She swept her startled gaze over the ripped guy behind the drums, twirling his sticks. He must be in his twenties. The middle-aged man seated at an electric organ plucked a few notes. Two remaining guys, one middle-aged, the other no more than eighteen, adjusted their guitars. Both had flutes slung at their sides like tomahawks. They wore headbands, long loose hair falling halfway down their backs, cut off t-shirts, upper arm tattoos, leather pants, and boots. Three of the men appeared Native American. The one at the organ didn't.

"What the heck, Jackson? No country western tonight?" She'd expected the fiddlers who'd played at her birthday bash.

"We change it up for Halloween." He pointed out the guitarist with gray streaking his black hair. "That's my Uncle Ray, Uncle Buck's older brother. You remember, my uncle from the hardware store in the valley?"

She almost had to prop her jaw shut. "Seriously?"

He crossed his heart.

"But I thought that particular uncle was banished for an unauthorized attack on humans?"

"*Attacks*, actually. And he was. But it's been years since the drunken ripping-out-throats spree Okema had to cover up, so he's allowing Uncle Ray back on probation. And his band, *Driving Nails,* is surprisingly not terrible."

"Super name." She peered through the crowd for a better look at the group. "What do they play?"

Jackson bent nearer. "Oh, the classic werewolf songs like *Werewolves of London*, *Lil Red Riding Hood*,

CCR's *Bad Moon Rising*...plus other rock stuff from the sixties and seventies."

She clapped her hands together. "Great! Aunt M. always liked the golden oldies, so I heard a lot of them growing up."

"Then you'll feel right at home." He waved at his uncle, who grinned and high-fived him from the impromptu stage. "And that's Ray's son, my cousin Rafe. He's their bass player." Jackson raised his fist in tribute to the youngest band member. Rafe enthusiastically returned the gesture, pumping the air. "Rafe means Counsel of the Wolf. I always thought that was cool." Jackson sounded wistful.

"Yeah, but I can't picture you as a Rafe." She studied the muscular drummer with a red bandana twisted into a head band, wavy brown hair brushing his beefy shoulders, and a sleeveless t-shirt that displayed his thick, corded arms. He had a dignified, almost regal presence, and wore a large medallion on a silver chain around his neck. "Who's that and what's on his emblem?"

"The head of a bear. He goes by Mato. It means bear in Lakota. He's a bearwalker."

She caught herself before uttering, 'Seriously' again. "Wow. That's awesome. How does bearwalking work?"

"Different from us, but there are similarities." Jackson hailed the drummer, who lifted his sticks in greeting. "Mato chooses when and where he wants to go as a bear. It's a mind thing few can master. He's part Shawnee and Lakota Sioux."

"Cool." Morgan held Mato in high esteem.

"Can't neglect Joe. He works with Ray at the

store." Jackson signaled the organist, sporting a blue baseball style cap with the hardware store logo on it. He snapped him a military salute in return. "That's Joe for you. He's quit or Ray's fired him half a dozen times, but they're stuck with each other." Jackson dropped his voice so no one but Morgan could hear. "Joe says he's a great warlock, but Hawth and I've never witnessed him do any magic. We think he hates being the only non-shifter in the band, so came up with that angle. If he was as powerful as he claims he is, Okema would ban him."

She surveyed the nondescript man with a graying mustache, grizzled chin, and the beginnings of a beer gut. Reddish-gray hair worn in a scruffy ponytail dipped below his cap, and he appeared of average height and build. "He doesn't look witchified, but you can't tell for sure. Neither does Dilly, and Okema hasn't banned her."

"True." Jackson pursed his mouth the way he did when pondering something. "Maybe if Joe swore undying allegiance to the Wapicoli, Okema would allow him on board. Times are growing harder for the clan these days. Might be why he's letting Uncle Ray back on a trial basis. Rafe was never out."

Morgan slid her gaze from the band back to Jackson. "'Needs must', to quote Miriam. How choosy can Okema be with all the threats facing us?"

A smile showed Jackson's white teeth. "Glad to hear you say *us*."

Indignation needled her. "Well, of course I did."

Again, the pensive mood as he considered. "You were pretty set on being a Morcant back at Lilith's."

As if she needed her memory prodded. Her cheeks

warmed at the recollection. "I wasn't myself then."

"I realize that—"

"And I don't look myself now," she rushed on. "But I'm still me under all this glitter."

He entwined his fingers through hers. "I know, but tests may still arise. Don't forget where, or to whom, you belong." He was in dead earnest.

"I won't." She was a little wounded he had any doubts.

The dark eyes behind the mask gazed into hers. "It's like this; even after Ray was banished, he remained loyal to the clan. Rafe would support us in a heartbeat, and has. So has Mato. You can bet a big old bear charging at you isn't something anyone wants." Jackson rubbed his chin thoughtfully. "Joe won't betray us. Whether he'd fight for us, we have yet to learn. A war's brewing, Morgan. We must know who we can trust. Our lives, yours, Jimmy's, all depend on it."

"I hear you." She heaved a sigh.

"Sorry. I don't mean to be a downer. Look." He gestured at the band. "They're gonna play."

Ray nodded at the other three. Mato struck his sticks together and counted, "One, two—a one, two, three, four!" Ray and Rafe swung their arms, tossed their heads, and the band ripped into the instantly recognizable chords of *Born to be Wild*. Ray sang into the microphone in a deep, low voice. A distinctive sound, and not half bad.

"You're right, Jackson. They're pretty darn decent." She had to practically yell at him to be heard. "The strain on your limited electricity must be a killer, though, with the instruments, amps, mics, and whatever."

"We have a backup generator for such occasions, and the occasional blizzard!"

The band concluded the number with a grand flourish. She joined in the hearty applause. Jackson, Hawthorne, and some of the guys whistled and fist pumped. Kids jumped up and down.

*Werewolves of London* followed, with the partygoers howling "Aaahoo!" at the appropriate intervals. Considering half of them were werewolves, Morgan appreciated the irony.

Then, she couldn't believe it. "Is that *Whiter Shade of Pale*? I love that song!"

"Me too. They're not *Procol Harum*. But Joe's a hit on the organ." Jackson took her hand. "Wanna dance?"

Heat flushed through her. "If you aren't expecting anything fancy?"

"Nope. Just a regular slow dance."

Nothing was *regular* about this evening, but a slow dance with Jackson qualified as heaven. He led her to the center of the room where the others made space for the dancers, Hawthorne and Dilly among them. She savored every sacred second pressed against Jackson, her head tucked in the crook of his shoulder, their arms wrapping each other.

Bless Uncle Ray and *Driving Nails* for following that song with the piercingly sweet *Nights in White Satin*. Morgan and Jackson indulged in a second slow dance, ribbons of fire running through her. Ray and Rafe came into their own with the flute part in that richly romantic melody, nearly bringing her to tears. She wished they'd play both songs again, but supposed not everyone wanted slow and sweet. Batboy, for one.

Give him a good howling wolf number any time.

The band launched into *Thriller*, much to crowd's glee.

She and Jackson reluctantly unwound their arms and made for the refreshment table. They were enjoying tiny sausages in cheesy pastry, cookies and punch, and shouted conversation with Hawthorne and Dilly, when the group started playing *Staying Alive* by the Bee Gees.

"Appropriate," she said, between fruity gulps.

Jackson jerked up his head. He tensed, sniffing the air, and darted his eyes at the room. "More than you know."

"Yeah." Hawthorne did the same. Dilly looked worried.

*What did they smell?* Apprehension mounting, Morgan breathed in, scouring the air.

Singling out an odor was difficult when it was masked by so many others. Everyone, especially those who weren't entirely human, had an animal musk mixed with their unique signature. Perfumes, like the one Dilly had doused her with, competed with the aromas of food, wood smoke, and candles. But Morgan also detected a familiar scent in the meld, one she'd sniffed before. Not long ago.

Alarm seized her, and she gripped Jackson's arm. "Where?"

Jaw clenched, he thumbed across the room. "There."

Chapter Twelve
Party Crashers

Striding through the door, pushing past startled partygoers grabbing children aside, was the last person Morgan expected to see. *Uncle Don.*

At least, she thought it was Uncle Don. He was big and blond with the prominent, but not too prominent nose, and chin. Fair, freckled, features like Jimmy's.

That's where the resemblance ended. He'd ditched the glasses, as if he no longer needed them, and his manner was anything but that of the mild librarian from before. His eyes flashed blue and he had fangs in his sneer.

The uncle she'd known never sneered, and he certainly didn't have fangs. His heavy plaid shirt, jeans, and hiking boots weren't out of place for a guy who also enjoyed the outdoors, but they were mud-spattered and frayed, like he'd waded through creeks and underbrush to get here. Relentlessly.

"God help us. It's him, the howl in the woods on our way back from Lilith's. He followed us," she croaked, clamping a hand to her mouth.

"Yeah. I get that now," Jackson muttered. "There's something I should have mentioned earlier, but I didn't want to alarm you. Morcant men don't make good werewolves."

"That's if they survive the change." Hawthorne's

voice was as tight as Morgan's chest.

Fear for Jimmy ratcheted beside horror of her violently altered uncle. Fortunately, the kid was shielded in metal, except for the opening at his eyes, nose, and mouth. He'd been stuffing cupcakes, but ceased. Like the rest of them, he lowered his plate to the table. Dilly simply vanished.

The formidable male, barely recognizable as their kin, halted in the center of the room. He was always tall, but appeared larger now. The band stopped and all eyes riveted on him. Warning rumbled from many throats. He'd entered the wolf den. Women and children scrambled back while the men closed rank. They'd shift. Then all hell would break loose.

*God no! Not here. Not now.* With small kids present, not to mention all the trouble everyone had gone to for the party. This room was sacred. They'd trash it. Still frozen, her hand to her mouth, Morgan hardly dared to breathe.

Uncle Don ignored his bitingly cold reception and the narrow, glittering eyes fixed on him. He swept his own scathing glare over the assembly. "I've come for my niece. I know she's here. Morgan! Where are you?"

"You're kin to him?" Dilly squeaked, reappearing somewhere behind her.

Morgan hated to admit it.

Gesturing for the other Wapicoli to stay back, Jackson stepped between her and the brazen intruder. "I don't know how you got past my grandma, Mr. Daniel. If she's hurt, you'll pay dearly. You're not welcome here. I strongly suggest you go."

"You think I came alone?" He waved at the rough men pouring through the door. Morgan couldn't see them clearly, but they smelled rank. There were at least half a dozen gamey intruders.

He must've found the enemy werewolves moving into Wapicoli territory and made himself alpha of the renegades. Never in a million years could she have seen that one coming.

Tension in the room tripled. This would get ugly fast. What a night to leave the door unbolted. And what of Miriam? Was she hurt? *Or worse*. Cold fear twisted Morgan's gut.

"I'm here." Miriam glided into the room in her tall black hat, and relief washed over Morgan.

"See? She's fine." Uncle Don stabbed a clawed finger at Jackson. "Now give me my niece, and we'll be gone."

Jackson was unyielding. "She stays."

"Your choice, or hers?" Uncle Don hissed.

He bristled. "Both. You just want her in your pack. If you truly cared for your family, you'd ask for Jimmy, too."

"Keep the boy. He's of no use to me. Morgan has real power."

She cringed to think how his disdain would hurt Jimmy.

Uncle Don sidled to Jackson's left, to try and see around him. His intent gaze searched the crowd. "She's seventeen by now and undergone the change. Where is she?"

Did he actually not realize it was her? Dilly's disguise was of benefit after all, and she was drenched in scent, not her own. Challenging Uncle Don here and now was the last thing Morgan wanted. Was it right to leave him to Jackson, though?

The hands Jackson clenched at his side were shifting. "Much as I'd love to reunite you with your dear niece, the clan and I are gonna show you and your pack to the door."

All around her, men were turning. A large brown bear now stood by the drums, and the guitarist and bass player were gray and tan wolves. Joe the Sorcerer looked on with slitted eyes, his arms upraised, as if he was about to zap Uncle Don. Whether it was because his gig had been rudely disrupted or he sided with the Wapicoli, she wasn't sure.

Snarls and snapping broke out on both sides. Frightened children were crying. She'd better decide fast whether to change and fight, or help the kids get away. She'd be the glitteriest werewolf ever.

"Enough!" Okema's voice rang out before he appeared, reminding Morgan she never knew exactly where he was.

The chief materialized in the center of the room, his aura so blindingly bright she blinked. His long white hair was dazzling, and the gold feathers knotted in the braids on top of his head were beams of light. He might be an eagle ready to soar into the heavens with sweeping wings, or a wind on the verge of a mighty blow.

His origins with the Star People shone forth. *This* was the being she'd sensed lay beneath his normally controlled exterior. He'd powered up. Only a very foolhardy soul would dare defy him. The Wapicoli fell silent in his presence. Uncle Don's pack stilled, but he didn't notice.

Outrage distorted his hard face. "You!" he spat out, with more venom in that single accusation than she thought possible.

Okema's silvery eyes flashed warning. "Yes. Me."

Uncle Don waved claws at him. "Thief! You stole my niece!"

Steel smoldered in Okema's gaze. "No thievery. She swore an oath of loyalty to the Wapicoli."

Uncle Don reared back his head, lips curled over his fangs. "Never! She's a Morcant!"

Morgan stepped shakily from behind Jackson and braced herself at his side. "I did, Uncle. I'm with the clan now. I'm terribly sorry for what's befallen you, but you must go."

His scotching eyes blistered her where she stood. "You traitorous, ungrateful—" Breaking off, he gaped at her. "What the hell have they done to you?"

She drew herself up. "It's Halloween, or didn't you notice?"

Again, he sneered. "It must be, to have you looking like *Princess Fu Fu*. Have they brainwashed you, girl?"

"No." She lifted her chin. "I choose to stand with the Wapicoli."

No point in explaining about Okema's offer of protection if she fought with them, or her falling in love with Jackson. Uncle Don's face was a mask of fury.

"You crazy backstabbing little—"

Before her incensed uncle finished the curse on his wounding tongue, Okema raised commanding hands. Blue flames crackled from his fingertips. "You have her answer. Take your pack and go, Morcant male. When next we meet, it will be to the death. *Yours,* if you continue on this path."

Fear crossed Uncle Don's neon-blue gaze, and Morgan scented it in the cold sweat of his rank wolfmen. "Come on," he barked to the others. "We'll deal with the Wapicoli later." He stabbed a finger at her. "As for you—"

A flick of Okema's hand sent Uncle Don hurdling backwards as if stuck by lightning. "I will not warn you twice."

If he lit into him with both hands, what would happen? Uncle Don must not want to discover. Getting to his feet, he staggered back the way he'd come with his bolting pack.

"Morgan!" A petite blonde woman she hadn't noticed in the tumult, broke free and rushed at her. Tears streamed down dirty, bruised cheeks, scratched by branches, and her clothes were torn. "Sanctuary, Okema! Take me in, I beg you!" She hurled herself into Morgan's arms. "My dear girl!"

"Aunt Maggie?" She hugged her dazedly, the familiar scent of home and family in her nostrils.

"It's me." Sobs heaved in her chest.

Pity surged alongside astonishment. What had she endured to reach her?

Lifting her head, Aunt M. swiveled streaming eyes at the stunned gathering. "Where's my Jimmy boy? Is he OK?"

"Yes!" He ran to her in a clank of metal, and the three of them held each other for dear life.

"It'll be all the worse for you, Maggie! This isn't over," Uncle Don threatened, from his retreat up the hall.

She shuddered, and Jackson clasped her shoulder. "He can't hurt you here, Ms. Daniel."

Red-hot anger permeated the room. Warriors fully changed, or partly shifted, growled deep in their throats.

Peter and Buck Wapicoli had charged in from the kitchen during the melee, and they were mad.

Peter slid his fiery gaze from Aunt M. to Okema. "Let's get him, and his pack."

"No. Let them go, for now," Okema ordered. "We'll attack at the first sign of trouble. Some may flee our territory. All will fight if cornered. I allow a Morcant one chance." He turned to the distraught woman. "I knew you would come, Maggie Daniel. What took you so long?"

"I've been locked in my cabin for two weeks by that lunatic! I broke free this afternoon and tailed him and that awful pack here. It's my fault. I know it's all my fault," she gasped. "I never should've bitten Don, but he's gone insane."

"It is the way with Morcant males," Okema said quietly.

She wiped a torn sleeve across her stained face. Scratches on her arm showed through the ripped cloth. "Why?"

He regarded her steadily. "The women in your clan are stronger. They better survive the change and withstand the effects."

"Here." Miriam's pressed a clean handkerchief into Aunt M.'s bruised and bloodied hand. When she'd stepped beside them, Morgan didn't know, but was glad for her support.

"There may be a cure." Miriam's calm assertion kindled a faint hope.

Okema exchanged glances with the wise healer. "And there may not be."

Chapter Thirteen
And the Band Stayed On

It wasn't every day a girl heard *In-A-Gadda-Da-Vida* while eating breakfast in a colonial era kitchen with fellow werewolves, descendants of the Star People, Mato, an esteemed bearwalker, Joe, a self-proclaimed warlock, and Dilly, the ditzy witch who hadn't yet figured out what she was. In fact, this was the first, possibly, only occasion.

*Man*, Jackson's Uncle Ray was really into the classic sixties rock song. Kind of a tough number to perform alone without the rest of the band who'd rather eat.

To give Ray credit, he wasn't doing a bad job, perched on a stool in the corner, bent over his acoustic guitar. He seemed oblivious of his surroundings. Even so, Morgan hated to disturb the rapt musician. Were they supposed to breakfast in silence while he jammed, or converse quietly amongst themselves?

Ray's cute son, Rafe, probably knew the proper protocol for the occasion. The teen sat on the bench across the table from her, between cousins Jackson and Hawthorne. Jimmy squeezed in on Hawth's left next to the noble bearwalker, wowed to devour bacon and eggs alongside the band, especially Mato. Jimmy had greeted Mato with an improvised ceremonial bow, probably one he'd picked up from some martial arts movie. The kid was awed when the most honored bearwalker returned his greeting. Then Mato divulged the band's secret *slap, slap, chop, chop, pound it* handshake, forever cementing himself in Jimmy's high regard.

Morgan signaled Rafe. "Is your dad doing the short or extended version of the song?" she asked quietly.

Humor in his surprisingly green eyes, Rafe waved aside her concern. "The seventeen minute one, and he improvises. Don't wait on him to finish. Go ahead and talk."

Clearly, Ray's solo fest was familiar ground.

Mato shook his head in faint amusement, wavy brown hair falling around his bearlike shoulders beneath the red bandana he'd twisted into a headband. The long-sleeved white Henley concealed his medallion and thick, hairy arms. Probably best at breakfast. The dude was seriously a beast.

He leveled his chocolate-colored gaze at her. "Wait until Ray does the drums."

She tried to imagine how that would work. "With his hands, on the sides of the guitar?"

"Yep." Mato knocked back a swallow of black coffee, and elbowed Joe. "Think he'll do the organ?"

Annoyance creased the avowed warlock's weathered face. "I darn well know Ray'll hum the freakin organ part. One of these days, I swear I'm gonna smack him into next week."

Dilly giggled from where she stood at the sink washing pots and pans. *Pulling her weight*, as she'd promised Okema.

Jackson winked at Morgan. Her heart fluttered the way it did most anytime he caught her eye. He was used to this back and forth between the guys. "Come on, Joe.

You can't blame Uncle Ray for preferring rock to selling ratchet sets."

"Suppose not," Joe grunted, "but he's not getting to Nashville on his lonesome."

*Half-decent* wasn't good enough to get any of them to Nashville, but Morgan didn't comment. Jackson smothered another grin, or tried.

Miriam turned from the hearth with a steaming platter of pancakes. "What I'm wondering is who's minding the store while you boys are away?"

"Mama," Rafe answered off-handedly. "It's bow season, so we're not too busy. A lot of men are off deer hunting."

"Give Doris our best when you see her." Miriam plunked the inviting platter beside the jug of maple syrup.

"Yes, ma'am. I will. She sends her regards." Rafe was as polite as the other young Wapicoli males—right up until they ripped someone apart, if the wolf got the better of them.

Mato speared two hotcakes with his fork. "I don't work at the store. I'm an independent contractor."

Rafe snorted. "Which means he does whatever he likes."

Morgan raised her coffee cup to Mato in a toast, seconded by Jimmy with his glass of milk. "Living the dream."

"Yeah. Isn't he." Jackson leaned on his elbow, head propped on one hand. They'd had a late night cleaning up after the party, and his energy level resembled Morgan's. Plus, she was still picking off glitter. "Has *Driving Nails* had many gigs lately?"

Rafe lifted one shoulder and let it drop, his long

hair held in place by the red rocker headband he and his father still wore. "Couple of weekends a month. Dad wants to take us on the road next summer. Do some fairs, that kind of thing."

Morgan wasn't sure people would flock in droves to hear them, but she admired their ambition.

"Lofty." Jackson echoed her sentiment. "Even winning *The Voice* would be easier than what lies before us, though."

Eyes thoughtful, Mato pondered. When he opened his mouth, everyone listened. "Want some help?" he asked. "I'm not in a tearing hurry to get back."

"Heck yeah!" Hawthorne pounced. "You know Santiago, don't you?"

Mato poured an amber stream onto his pancakes. "Some. I've been to his place a few times. Had a beer with the dude."

Jackson saluted him. "That's more than can be said for us. We tend to steer clear of those wildcats. But we need to meet with Santiago ASAP."

"Why now?" Mato pressed, the others looking on.

Hawthorne thumbed at Dilly. "Her mama spelled Jimmy last week."

Her hands sudsy, Dilly spun around. "I'm real sorry about that!"

"I know." Waving aside her apology, Jackson continued. "Problem is, Lilith won't undo the spell until we deliver the serpent's fang Santiago wears around his neck."

"Is that all," Mato said drily.

"No biggie." Rafe had a sarcastic edge to his tone.

"Really? Shoot." Joe slid bluish-gray eyes between them. "How long has the kid got until the spell kicks in?"

"Until the next full moon." Jimmy's robotic reply wasn't encouraging.

Every head turned toward him. "He answers like that each time he hears any reference to the spell," Morgan explained, with the usual sinking sensation.

"It's the dern Panther Moon coming up," Rafe muttered. "Not exactly in our favor."

Morgan made a mental note to ask Jackson to explain.

Joe frowned beneath his blue cap. "You're a powerful bunch. Can't you make this witch recant?"

Dilly flung up her soapy hands and wailed. "Mama's real set on her spells once she's done 'em. And she can be awful spiteful when crossed."

Mato chewed, intent on every word. He washed his pancake down with strong black coffee. "What are you offering Santiago in return for his treasure? It had better be good."

"Oh, it is." Jackson circled fingertips at his forehead, as if easing an ache. "An alliance. We'll cease hostilities toward the Mountain Panteras, if they do the same, and join with them to fight Mateo. Together, we may drive him and his gang from these mountains. Think Santiago will go for it?"

Another swig of coffee, and Mato shrugged. "He might. Santiago's tired of losing men to Mateo. He might just as easily refuse, too."

Morgan bent toward Mato. "Would Santiago be more amenable with your influence? Surely, having you negotiate would help?"

"Maybe. I'll give it a shot." For a long moment, he scrutinized her. "You might also have a chance with him. He's partial to a pretty face."

"Sure," she nodded, not at all certain of such a meeting. "If you think I can help Jimmy. I'll talk to him."

Jackson frowned. "I don't much like that idea."

"Let me make contact with Santiago first," Mato suggested. "Then see who he's willing to hear. I'll ask to sit in, and you'd be close by, Jackson."

"You bet I will. Ready to storm the fortress if need be."

"In a nanosecond," Hawthorne inserted. "As will I."

"I'll go along, if you want more backup," Rafe offered.

Jackson clasped his shoulder. "Sure do. *Megwich.* We don't know what we're up against."

Joe crossed his arms over his chest, covered in a flannel shirt. "I'm in. A warlock might come in handy."

"Yeah. Anybody see one?" Ray laid his guitar on his lap.

"Funny. Only I'm not laughing." Joe wore a broody look.

"Fine. Prove yourself then. Set something on fire with your eyes, or zap someone," Ray challenged.

"How about you?" Joe suggested, rubbing a grizzled chin.

"Still waiting." Ray turned to Jackson. "I'm in on this quest thing, too. If you want me."

"Of course we do. You and Joe both." Jackson held up a silencing hand. "Head count. I'm guessing Dilly wants to go?"

She bobbed her red head. "Absolutely."

"And Jimmy kind of has to come along, for Lilith

to undo the spell. So that's another," Morgan interjected.

"Right." Lips twitching, Jackson ran his gaze around the circle. "That makes nine of us in—wait for it—the *Fellowship of the Fang*."

Hawth burst out laughing. "Oh dude, that is so bad."

Rafe pounded the table. "Man, you're killing me."

Even Mato smiled. The two older men rolled their eyes. Miriam and Willow silently shook their heads, as if they'd heard it all now.

Ray accepted a hot mug of coffee from Miriam. "What about Peter and Buck? Any chance of Okema coming?"

"I wish. Okema wants to see how we can get on without him." Jackson's humor dimmed. "In case…we have to before long."

"I sure hope not," Ray said somberly. "He was mighty powerful last night."

"Yeah." Jackson's lips tightened. He must be as intimidated as Morgan, wondering how they could ever take Okema's place. "Dad and Uncle Buck will come if we want, but we can't leave the lodge unguarded." Jackson didn't add, 'with Morgan's crazy uncle on the prowl,' but it was implied.

"Gotcha." Ray took his meaning. He swallowed the fragrant brew, then waved his mug at the assembly. "Well kids, when do we make a start?"

Jackson eyed Morgan questioningly. He was well aware of her worry over Aunt M., still asleep as far as she knew. Dilly was bunking in with Morgan now, so Aunt M. could have her former cot in Miriam's bedroom. The kindly healer had ministered to the embattled newcomer. The last Morgan had seen of Maggie Daniel she was clean, her cuts soothed with balm, and she'd sunk into the oblivion of the utterly exhausted.

It could take several days for Aunt M. to recover, and after that, Morgan wasn't sure what she'd do. Meanwhile, they had to get on with their mission. She gave Jackson a nod.

He smoothed back his hair. "The sooner we go, the better. How about first thing in the morning? Gives us today to recuperate and prep. We'll have to swing by Lilith's after the deed's done."

"Assuming Santiago buys into this," Mato reminded him, not that anyone was taking a deal with him for granted.

Setting his mug on the sideboard, Ray thrummed his guitar dramatically. "It'll be hours if we hike there. Want to take the truck on this quest? Mine's available."

Mato drummed on the table with his fork. "And mine."

"I'd offer you one, bro, but I'm truckless," Rafe said.

Jackson high-fived him. "It's the thought. I'd like four-wheelers or dirt bikes for these backroads, but Okema has nixed them. Trucks will be great. Thanks, guys." The sheen in his eyes revealed the depth of his appreciation for their offer. A potentially risky one, fraught with danger.

"Nine there are going forth from the lodge," Morgan said softly. "I hope nine return."

Hawthorne snapped to attention. "Oh, good. Are we doing *Fellowship of the Fang* again?" He thumped the right side of his chest with his fist, then extended his palm toward Jimmy in the chivalrous sign of a pledge. "By all that's sacred, I swear to protect you, small one. You have my badass sword."

Jimmy gave him a look. "You would choose Aragorn."

"I noted that too." Jackson swept his hand at Jimmy. "And you have my awesome bow," he adlibbed, Legolas style.

"And my amazing ax," Mato intoned the guttural accents of Gimli, the fierce dwarf. "Except, it's a tomahawk."

"Whatever." A pause, and Hawthorne gestured impatiently at Rafe. "Come on, man. Someone's got to do Boromir."

"Great. The loser who gets himself killed. Okay. Okay." Adjusting his expression, Rafe gazed earnestly at batboy. "You carry the fate of us all, little dude. By heaven, if this is the will of the council, then Gondor's on board." He followed his avowal with a bow.

"And me." Dilly scanned the circle, her expression puzzled. "Where are we going again?"

Hawthorne grinned. "We've got our Pippin!"

"I'm making the wild guess I'm Frodo." Jimmy pursed his lips. He'd prefer a role that involved swords or bows.

"You're the obvious *Halfling* in the fellowship." Hawthorne was loving this.

Joe perked up and his mustache twitched. "Does that make me Gandalf?"

"No. *He's* staying behind." Ray referred to Okema. "Seriously, guys. This is gonna take some doing to pull off."

An air of solemnity stilled the banter. They knew.

The fooling around was their way of easing the tension.

"Any good luck charms, Grandma?" Jackson asked.

Wiping floury hands on her apron, Miriam pivoted toward them, the hearth illuminating her from behind. "I'll make you each something to carry in your pockets. Stay focused on your mission. Do as Mato says and send him in first to request a parley with Santiago. Likely, Morgan would be a good choice to negotiate."

*Not alone*? Her heart dropped into her leaden stomach, but she steeled herself for what lay ahead.

Miriam's attention was fixed on her. "Remain calm, but firm when you speak with him. Remind him what he has to gain, not what he's forfeiting." A shadow clouded her gaze, and she swiped a white streak across her beaded forehead. "I wish I knew what Lilith wants with that serpent's fang."

"What does any witch want?" Mato queried, knowingly.

"Power." Miriam weighed Dilly. "Well, usually."

Dilly didn't seem the least bit power mad. She sank onto a vacant stool, absently twisting her apron. "I don't have a clue what Mama wants with some old snake's tooth. It's gross."

Miriam seemed to see past them, as if her farsighted vision searched Lilith's mind. "I can't think how this fang will bring her power, but I fear it may. Meanwhile, all you can do is proceed as planned. Stay sharp and beware."

Warning tolled in Morgan.

## Chapter Fourteen
Pirate's Lair

Although it was closer to noon, the shrouded woods had an eerie twilight feel. Slanting glances from side to side and over her shoulder, Morgan sat on the tailgate of Ray's truck with Jackson, his Uncle Ray, Rafe, and Jimmy. Hawthorne, Dilly, and Joe perched on the back of Mato's parked truck. Everyone conversed at a low hum.

Ray's vehicle angled in one direction, and Mato's in another, to better keep watch. The *Fellowship of the Fang* was stalled while they awaited word from the bearwalker, meeting with Santiago inside his red and yellow gypsy-styled wooden caravan. Hazy tendrils entwined the unlikely home on wheels.

So much for hopes of a sunny, blue sky day. If a potential encounter with Santiago wasn't nerve-racking enough, Morgan feared her crazed uncle might spring at them from the mist at any moment. Being bitten must've been kind of like contracting rabies for him. Nothing else made any sense, assuming sense entered into any of this.

Granted, she'd gotten Wandering Wolf, but hadn't gone insane. Thank God she'd left that bizarre episode behind her—with help.

*Dratted moon curse.* Was there a treatment for Uncle Don? Or would they have to put him down like a rabid dog? Miriam wasn't specific concerning a cure, and Morgan cringed at the alternative.

Why were Morcant males so susceptible, anyway?

Okema hadn't said, only that they were. The mystifying chief had warned Uncle Don away, but that didn't mean he'd obey him, and stay at bay. She sniffed the autumn woods for any hint of his presence, her ears tuned to every sound.

At least, she didn't look like a total dork on this quest, like the last one. She was exceedingly glad to be dressed in her customary leather jacket and form-fitting pants, hiking boots, the brown knitted cap on her head. A long-sleeved thermal shirt added another layer for warmth.

*Snap*. She startled at a cracking twig, flipping her blond ponytail as she whipped toward the sound.

"Easy. Only a deer. Might've heard a chipmunk, too." Jackson passed her the thermos of cocoa they shared, his breath white in the frosty air. "We're ready for a sudden attack. As ready as we can be, anyway."

She relaxed slightly.

He was armed—they all were—with bows on or beside them. Her weaponized scarf was knotted at her throat; a sheathed knife hung from the belt at her waist. Most of the guys had slung tomahawks at their sides. Their greatest weapon, though, lay in who and what they were.

Ray sipped from his thermos, coffee for him, and swiped the sleeve of his camouflage hunting jacket across his mouth. He studied her from beneath his camo cap, appearing for all the world like an ordinary hunter, which he was, plus a werewolf. "Always prepare for the expected and the unexpected. As to the outcome—" His low voice dropped off.

She took a nervous swallow of the hot, chocolaty drink Miriam had thoughtfully provided. "That's the whole problem. The uncertainty."

Jimmy drank from his zombie themed school thermos and bit into a leftover cupcake from the party. He'd stuffed his pack full, not taking any chances of running low on food again. Neither was Hawthorne, distributing snacks to his truck buddies. "Wanna call in the elves for backup?" Jimmy asked, his voice muffled by the cupcake. "They're handy with a bow."

"Sure, Frodo. There might actually be some out here. The scenery kind of reminds me of the elven forest in Middle-earth. Not those, though." She gestured at the caravans with her gloved hand, the bright colors of the homes on wheels bold in the fog. "Why didn't anyone tell us the Mountain Panteras live like gypsies? I thought they denned up in caves?"

"Not all," Jackson amended. "The men take turns guarding the treasure. There." He subtly indicated the dark opening in the rocks veiled in mist not far from where they'd parked. Smoke trailing from the cave's mouth indicated a fire burning within. Someone had to tend the blaze. "Awhile back, these Panteras mixed with a band of gypsies, which accounts for the culture meld."

"Quite a meld. I sure didn't expect to find the Panteras living in a cluster of caravans." Some of the handcrafted homes were bow shaped with a rounded front opening like the covered wagons that headed west, only far more colorful. Others had straight sides with small windows and curved tops. Equally eye-catching.

Each mini dwelling was uniquely painted; red, yellow, blue, purple, and silver among the dominant hues. Heavy embellishment, images and designs that had no meaning for her, almost entirely covered some of the caravans. Smoke rose from the small stovepipes in the roofs.

She envisioned bunk beds, cupboards, a quaint cook stove, shiny pots and pans...all cozily tucked inside. A place for everything and everything in its place. "You've gotta admire their talent. Quite the Suzy homemakers, aren't they?"

"Hardly." Jackson accepted a second cupcake from Jimmy, as did everyone except her. "Don't get the warm fuzzies and underestimate them for a second. They've dug tunnels throughout these trees and have secret passages in the cavern. They're everywhere. Waiting, watching. Pouncing."

"Oh." Her stomach too knotted for treats, she scanned the woods and rocky outcroppings. "So there are more of them than it seems, judging from the caravans?"

"Many," Rafe confirmed, between bites, his eyes shaded by the wide-brim of a chestnut-colored fedora similar to the ones Jackson and Hawthorne wore.

Ray inclined his capped head. "A wolf likes to feel the wind in its face, with easy to exit dens. Not Panteras. They don't object to dense stone surrounding them on every side, or tunneling deep under the earth. Gypsies prefer aboveground dwellings, though. That required some compromise."

Dark eyes in dusky faces peered at them from the curtained windows in some of the homes on wheels. "So the Mountain Panteras accommodated both inclinations?"

"Gypsies are the original tiny house people. Panteras simply adapted." Jackson brushed crumbs off his leather coat.

Like cats, who could live inside or out, she supposed.

The unseen eyes she also sensed watching them made her skin crawl. "What do they do for money? Apart from the treasure?"

Jackson observed their visible onlookers. "They eke that out. Panteras hate parting with gold. So do gypsies, for that matter. They're artisans, kind of like us, and turn up at some of the same craft shows. We have an unspoken agreement not to attack each other in public. Bad for business. They're also expert hunters, and live off the land. They used to keep horses to pull their caravans. Nowadays, it's trucks."

The outline of pickups was visible in the whiteness. She kind of wished they still had horses.

Ray capped his thermos. "But the cave is never left unguarded. Some men stay. Some go. They rotate sentry duty."

"How many are there, total?" she wondered aloud.

"We never took a headcount." Jackson swept his hand at their surroundings. "How could we?"

She saw his point. "If Santiago agrees to an alliance with us, how do we tell him and his pack apart from Mateo's?"

Jackson eyed her in surprise. "I thought you realized. These Panteras are orangey-gold when they shift."

Her thoughts traveled back to when she'd been laid up. "Then the orange panther I glimpsed in the flames of my bedroom hearth wasn't only from the fever?"

"A vision of what was to come," he suggested.

"Sent by Grandma Sarah, maybe," she mused. "That means Mateo's gang are the black panthers. Why the difference between them?"

Lifting his hands in an 'I don't know' gesture, Jackson shrugged. "Never had the chance to ask."

Ray leaned in. "Maybe they were always this way, and the two groups at odds to begin with. Could partly account for the original split eons ago when they fell out."

Surrounding heads nodded.

"Like warring wolf packs." She had another thought. "How do I tell them apart if they *haven't* shifted yet?"

"You'll see. Different hair styles, manner of dress, accents..." Jackson trailed off as Mato emerged from the caravan onto the small front stoop and descended the three steps to the leafy earth.

The red bandana still wrapped around his head like a headband. A large green canvas coat reached knee-length on his jeans, with a narrow gap between the faded denim and his leather boots. He walked toward them, a glower on his face. "Santiago agreed to meet with you, Morgan. And *only* you." He nodded toward the cave Jackson had pointed out. "In there."

"Super." An assignation in their doggone lair all on her lonesome. "No tête-à-tête in the cozy caravan over tea and crumpets," she muttered.

Jackson closed a reassuring arm around her. "We're right here, Morgan. You know how fast we can move."

Especially him. However, he and the others rushing

to her aid depended on her ability to utter a cry from inside that dank hole—in time. She was pretty much entering the lion's den alone. She'd need plenty of courage for this.

"What's Santiago like?" she whispered.

"A pirate," Jackson, Rafe, and Ray answered in unison.

Jimmy refrained from adding, 'Duh.' Probably because his mouth was too full, and Hawthorne out of earshot.

His expression thunderous, Mato stopped by the back of the truck. "Oh, and their mighty leader said to leave all weapons behind."

"I will." Except for the scarf, and her innate ability, and it was this that mattered most. "It's OK, man. You did your best. *Megwich*," Morgan offered, in an attempt to assuage Mato's guilt. At the very least, he'd wanted to accompany her.

He thumbed his finger at the caravan. "Mr. Badass is super brave. Only willing to meet with a girl."

"I'm not gonna go belly up, if that's what he thinks. Does Santiago know I'm the Seventh Morcant?"

Mato arched his brows, then furrowed them and stared at her hard. He clapped a hand to his forehead. "Of course. How stupid of me."

If he'd been unaware, chances were…

A faint chuckle escaped Jackson, despite everything, or perhaps because of their unusual circumstances. "I expect Santiago's about to find out. Power up, Wolf Girl."

"I intend to." She rubbed the moonstone at her throat under the wool scarf given to her by Grandma Sarah. She didn't fully know the magical gem's potential, but a tingle ran through her fingers.

Mindful of Miriam's contribution, she squeezed the small bundle in her pocket made of twigs from the sacred oak and cedar trees, bound together with fragrant sage stems, leaves, and pine needles. Whether it was the combination of the specially chosen plants, or her ties to Miriam, she couldn't say, but she was buoyed by both women's gifts.

"Time to go." She unbuckled her belt, leaving the knife behind. She'd already laid her bow aside, and deposited her quiver. "That's it." As far as the Panteras could tell.

Without overt weapons, she jumped down off the tailgate near Mato. Jackson landed beside her, his footfall muffled. Rafe, Ray, and Jimmy followed them. Hawthorne, Dilly, and Joe took the cue and joined the huddle forming around Morgan.

She scanned their faces, some muted beneath wide brims. Hope hinted in Mato's eyes, kind of like he'd realized she was 'the slayer.' Jimmy's hooded jacket outlined his chilled freckled cheeks. Concern creased the blue eyes behind his glasses. A parka encircled Dilly's rosy face, her blue-green gaze uncertain. Joe glowered beneath his blue cap, and puffed out his mustache. Everyone was intent on Morgan.

*What a moment.* She could be the star quarterback, but her quest better suited Gandalf. "One thing I want to make clear. No matter what, we are not leaving without that fang."

"Never thought we were," Joe grunted.

"The fellowship stands firm." Jackson clasped her shoulder, and Hawthorne gripped her other. Ray repeated the gesture with Rafe and Jimmy. Gloved hands reached out, grasping shoulders or arms—whatever they could reach—until the circle was completely linked.

If she didn't feel empowered before, she did now. "For Jimmy."

"For Jimmy," echoed the gathering.

"For Jimbo," Jackson said.

Tears winked in the kid's eyes. She'd never seen him so touched, or quiet. So quip-less.

Guarding emotion from overtaking her, Morgan looked at Jackson. He gave her a nod.

No one said a word as she reluctantly broke the circle, turned away, and strode toward the cave. Their silent support was more fitting. How many Panteras were inside, or when Santiago would make an appearance, was anybody's guess. As far as she could tell, he hadn't yet left his caravan.

Resolve welled in her. If only one shifter emerged from that dark hole, it was gonna be her. And she wasn't exiting empty-handed.

Chapter Fifteen
Blue Light Special

*Arrogant pirate*. How dare Santiago keep Morgan waiting like this? He was the key to the whole endeavor, and evident only by his absence. She was tempted to storm his caravan, and it wouldn't take a double dog dare, let alone a triple-dog, for her to do it. Too bad she couldn't teleport like Dilly. She'd already be there, savoring the shock on his smarmy face.

Fuming at the delay, she stood, arms folded across her chest, tapping the stone floor with a booted foot. She'd bet her comrades in the fellowship waiting by the trucks were none too pleased either. Maybe they'd drag Santiago out for her. If his aim was to antagonize her, he'd succeeded. Royally. Meanwhile, they were burning daylight, what little there was.

She loathed caves, and wasn't overly fond of Panteras. Finding herself confined with them in this rock carving leftover from the ice age was a trial. Sooty torches and the crackling fire illuminated her dismal surroundings and feral companions. Blackened walls bore witness to the campfire's continual use, probably since they first invaded these mountains on their retreat from the British Royal Navy several hundred years ago. Even in summer, this dank hole wouldn't be inviting. Unless you enjoyed hanging out in a tomb, which apparently they did, rather like vampires.

Dancing flames provided the only comfort, but she wasn't near enough to benefit from their warmth. She'd refused a seat in the circle, barely bitten back a 'Hell no.' Not very sociable of her, she supposed. The Panteras weren't giving off good vibes, or scents, though. Discarded whiskey bottles, and several men swigging from open flasks didn't help matters. Seems Lilith had faithful customers among them. Dealing with inebriated Panteras would be even more of a pain.

Half a dozen men were on guard duty, such as they were. Dark-haired males slouched in battered camp chairs around the fire in the center. Shadowed figures skulked in murky corners. An overhead draft, plus the opening in the entryway, lessened the pungent smoke, though her eyes still stung a bit. A smoky trail drifting into an unseen space behind her meant this cave was the first of many such cavernous rooms. Sinuous passages might wind through the whole freaking mountain.

*No thanks.* She had no desire to navigate that torturous route. It explained how Panteras appeared out of thin air in the middle of the woods.

This bunch sure weren't into camouflage. They must shift into panther form to conduct furtive patrols, or they'd be spotted as easily as someone yelling, 'Over here!'

The gypsy influence was apparent in the vivid shirts showing beneath their leather coats, and the flamboyant scarves at their necks, and on several heads. Maybe pirates were also big on flair. Come to think of it, they did have that reputation.

The men's black hair and eyes were a blend of Spanish and gypsy ethnicities. Admittedly attractive, if she didn't number them among her foulest enemies.

They wore their hair long, either loose, pulled back, in multiple narrow braids, or dreads. Some bound their hair with scarves the brilliant hues of a sunset. Gold hoops, studs, and cascading spangles glinted at their ears. Gold bands circled their wrists and rings shone on their fingers. Sapphires, rubies, and other precious gems embellished their finely crafted jewelry—worth a fortune.

She could guess where the goodies came from, but had no clue where they'd hidden the treasure. Nor did she care. Let them hoard it. Probably cursed anyway. Besides, that wasn't her aim in coming.

Panteras—not necessarily these—had killed her parents, Jackson's mother, grandfather, and Lord only knew how many others. She was here to negotiate, not tear their heads off. That didn't require her getting chummy with them. The oily musk they exuded, reminiscent of Mateo, further offended her. She should've worn a hazmat helmet.

Heck, her wolf scent might not appeal to her unwilling companions either. She was definitely getting a reaction from them. Some men watched her furtively. Others were far bolder, their roving eyes and mocking smiles not lost on her. She was tempted to wipe the smirks off their faces, and empty the remains of the whiskey over their heads. She'd do it, too.

*Time to reveal more of the wolf.* Let them know who they were dealing with. Not a helpless girl they could abuse. Let them try laying a finger on her.

Narrowing what she knew were now blistering blue eyes at her onlookers, she curled her lips over fangs. Heads jerked back, smiles fading. Some men retreated further into the shadows. Others returned her glare with eyes glinting tawny gold—meeting her warning with threats of their own.

*Make them respect you*, an inner voice directed. *Okema.*

*You know what to do*, he prompted.

*Yes.* She did. In a convoluted way, she was his protégé.

He'd inadvertently created the first Morcant with Sarah, after cursing her father for violating sacred Indian land. Sarah had saved her illustrious parent, but the curse had passed to her and generations of Morcant women. More than two centuries later, for better or worse, Morgan was the outcome.

Antagonism toward her was mounting in the cave. Throaty growls rumbled alongside the glittering stares. Several Panteras capped their flasks and set them aside. Some who'd been seated were slowly rising, like affronted felines ready to spring.

*Now*, Okema urged her, as he'd done before she realized from whom the psychic summons arose.

Either she acted immediately, or yelled loudly for help.

*Act, Morgan!*

Tapping into the current pulsing within her, she lifted her hands as she'd witnessed him do at the Halloween party. Unbelievably, and yet, not so unbelievable, blue light emanated from her fingers, through the brown gloves. Whether she could send anyone flying backwards as he'd done, remained to be seen.

Men gaped at her from chairs, crouched stances, and corners. Those still seated leapt to their feet. None wanted to be caught in a vulnerable posture.

*Ha*! She ran her gaze over the group. "Neat trick, huh? Only it's not a trick. You all know Okema?"

Slack-jawed, bristling with suspicion, they nodded.

"Heads-up. I get my power from him. Not sure how much yet. Shall we discover?" She flicked her fingers at a camp chair and it tumbled sideways. An encouraging start.

"A man weighs more," snarled one large Pantera, dressed in black and purple, a red scarf twisted over his dreadlocks, and ropes of gold necklaces around his thick neck.

"Yes. He does." Harnessing the current surging inside her, she pushed her hands in his direction. Energy sizzled through her fingers, and he staggered back. Not with the force Okema had zapped Uncle Don, but enough to send a thrill of confidence rippling down her spine.

Her onlookers were too dumbfounded to shift, or make a move. If they rallied, and rushed her at once, she'd be hard-pressed to fight them all off. Might even need backup in a hurry. Especially if they had guns, like Mateo and his gang. There were no visible assault rifles, but they might have revolvers tucked away. She wasn't up to deflecting bullets yet. As far as she knew, anyway.

Taking advantage of their confusion, she spoke again. "You're probably wondering why I called this meeting."

Brows shot up. "You?" A man argued. "It was Santiago."

"At my request," she clarified, making herself the dynamic in the unfolding scenario. "I grow tired of waiting. Which one of you is going to fetch him for

141

me?"

She flicked her fingers at the fire and the flames flared up responsively. *Sweet.* Maybe she could hurl a fireball across the cave.

Men exchanged nervous glances, probably wondering what else she could do. As was she.

While they were unprepared for her abilities, neither did they seem to care for the notion of fetching Santiago. A mood of reluctance came over them.

"Is he scarier than me?" She waved her hands and every camp chair flew back.

*Clapping.*

Who applauded her? Closing her startled mouth, she spun toward the tall lean figure entering the cave.

The man who must be Santiago didn't simply walk over the stone floor, he swaggered in fitted leather pants and high-topped pirate boots cuffed at the rim. A three-cornered leather hat crowned his head.

The tricorn appeared old enough to belong to his original, sailed-the-high-seas ancestor. Maybe it was. If he'd crossed paths with Morgan a few days ago, she'd have been wearing her colonial grandmother's clothes.

Santiago kind of resembled the man she pictured as *the Dread Pirate Roberts*, with devilishly good looks and killer eyes. Did he stick to some sort of pirate code?

Dark brown hair curled around his shoulders over a leather coat, vest, old-fashioned white shirt, and red scarf knotted at his throat. A tier of gold and ruby balls dangled from his ears. Jade comprised the large signet ring on his index finger featuring the head of a serpent, and he wore other jewel encrusted rings. A sword, possibly vintage, with a bejeweled hilt, and an antique pistol hung from the wide belt at his waist. As did a leather shot pouch. Was the pistol seriously a flintlock, black powder, muzzle loader?

*Wow*. He'd really gone all out on the eighteenth century pirate look. Most significant among his splendid array, was the large fang suspended from the silver chain around his neck.

A chill shivered through her. There it was.

*Whew*. You wouldn't want to accidentally stab yourself on that relic.

To prevent such an unfortunate occurrence from transpiring, the pointy end was encased in a silver cap engraved with an image of the fearsome creature from which it came. Obtaining the tooth in the first place must've been quite a feat. Maybe the serpent left it impaled in the ship's mast—or a Pantera—during the fierce battle. How had they escaped the sea monster? Maybe all of them hadn't.

The biggest 'how' involved her wrangling this prize away from such a diehard, cast from the past, Pantera. The sacred fang was likely the epicenter of his persona. She had some serious persuading to do.

All this, she absorbed in a second. Santiago now stood before her, and a head taller. He cast a long shadow.

Eyes glowing green, he brought his tanned hands together in a mock tribute. "Bravo, *Mujer Lobo*."

Her grasp of Spanish was sufficient enough to understand he'd called her 'Wolf Girl,' or a variation thereof, and she didn't like it coming from him. "English please. And let's stick with Morgan."

"As you wish." He swept her a bow in fake gallantry.

She gauged his insincerity, not only because they

were natural born enemies, but because his eyes should be dark brown or black, not the hue of neon playdough. A shifter only revealed his or her true colors when on the defensive or offensive, and she strongly suspected the latter with him. His calculating demeanor immediately made her tighten her defenses. This Pantera leader wouldn't be easily intimidated. Not that she was easy. Energy crackled in her. But who knew what crackled in Santiago?

If she seized his smug face between her hands, she'd incinerate him. But as Jackson had emphasized earlier about Mateo, a lot of sharp teeth, claws, slamming muscle, and pure cunning lay between her and that not so simple act. Santiago could shift in seconds. Though powered by the wolf, she'd need to remain in largely human form to carry out her agenda.

The men straightened at his arrival, newfound confidence in their bearing, as if they told themselves, 'All is well now.'

This is why, historically, you always cut off the head of the snake when dealing with opposing forces. Once the leader was down, the followers were far easier to eliminate, or obliged you by retreating. She was here to parley, not battle this particular serpent, but he also must be made to respect her, or she'd get nowhere fast.

Miriam's advice returned to her: *Stay focused on your mission. Remind him what he has to gain, not what he's forfeiting.*

*Very well.* Morgan flicked her hands at two chairs and magically righted them so they faced each other across the fire. "Shall we be seated and converse civilly?" she invited.

A spark of approval warmed Santiago's gaze and a

smile revealed white teeth. Waving his men back, he inclined his head. Some males remained emboldened, others were uncertain of Morgan, but every eye targeted her.

Another ducal bow, and her host gestured for her to be seated. "As you have so graciously restored our furnishings, let us begin."

His groupies remained at a respectful, but ready Freddie distance as the she-wolf and panther king lowered themselves into seats, taking each other's measure with the flames in between. What either one of them could or would do, could only be supposed. She knew little of pirates, but expected the worst. He had much to learn of her.

He interlocked his ringed fingers across his chiseled middle. "Why have you come to me?"

Mato must've given him a clue in their earlier meeting, but she bore with the formality of this parley. "To seek an alliance between the Mountain Panteras and the Wapicoli."

His gaze, a less molten green now, never left hers. "Why now?"

Willing the fire in her eyes to dim, she twirled a blond strand around a gloved finger. "For our mutual benefit. Do you not weary of Mateo's continual attempts to take what is rightfully yours, and the resulting toll upon your band?"

His expression hardened. "I do not deny he and his gang are a blight upon us."

"As they are on the Wapicoli," she said quietly.

He tilted his head, as if considering her from another angle. "How is it you speak for them? Why does Okema allow a woman such authority?"

Was Santiago testing her? "You scent the wolf within me. Do you not know who I am?"

"A Morcant. *Enemy* of the Wapicoli. And they of you." His forehead furrowed beneath the turned up brims of his hat. "Why ally yourself with them?"

"To gain Okema's protection of me and my younger brother." She didn't mention her intractable bond with Jackson, divulging only as much as necessary.

Santiago raised his hands, palms up, in a gesture of conciliation. "For you, this is reasonable. Why does the great chief have need of a Morcant woman?"

She summoned the sizzle back into her eyes. "I'm not just any Morcant."

His dark brows drew together. "So the legend is true?"

"It is," she affirmed. "Can you not see who sits before you?"

Rubbing a chin with a five-day-old beard, he nodded. "You glow blue. Not only your eyes. All of you."

"My aura?" She'd never heard this before.

"Yes." He shouldered back in his chair. "So, Seventh Morcant, your power is far greater than the others?"

"More than you can imagine." Praying it worked, she circled her fingers at the fire and sent flames rising in a bluish arch. "Are you convinced yet, or is this a common practice for you?"

Eyes like green marbles lit from within, he pinched his lips together, parting them to hiss. "Only Okema can do this."

"And me." And Jackson when he embraced his

birthright.

Flicking her fingers, she made the flames rise and fall. "Do you want me and the Wapicoli allied with the Mountain Panteras, or do you prefer to continue battling us and Mateo?"

A sneer twisted Santiago's otherwise handsome face. "That city Pantera and his gang ravage all. More than two centuries pass and they think to return and claim—steal—our portion of the treasure." He spat out his disgust, shared by the men intent on their conversation and her. Especially her.

"The Wapicoli have no interest in your treasure, Santiago."

He arched a quizzical brow. "What of you, Morgan Morcant?"

She shook her head.

A gesture for her to continue followed. "I am listening."

"Good." She allowed the fire to dwindle and bent nearer. "There's one other thing you should know. My uncle is a Morcant now in the full sense."

Frowning, Santiago argued. "I did not think that possible. Morcant males rarely survive the change."

Another reminder of how much she needed Okema's, and all the Wapicoli's, protection for Jimmy. "It has made Uncle Don crazed, and vowing vengeance, not only on the Wapicoli, but the Panteras. He leads a pack of rogue werewolves."

Clearly, this was new information. A skeptical gleam entered Santiago's scrutiny. "You would fight your own uncle to side with us?" He waved his hand at their avid audience, and broader, to encompass those outside. "All Mountain Panteras?"

She forced herself to focus solely on Jimmy. "If I must. But there is one condition you, in turn, must meet before we form an alliance." Gesturing at his necklace, she braced herself for a furious refusal. "The serpent's fang."

Never had she seen eyes glow that green. More than Hawthorn's kryptonite gaze when he was provoked or shifting. More like an alien species from another planet.

"No!" Santiago snapped his fingers around the precious relic. "Why should I part with it?"

Stilling the tremor threatening her voice, she answered calmly. "Lilith insists she must have the tooth or my brother perishes by her spell."

If looks could slay, Morgan would lie dead on the cave floor. "*This* is why you are here. *This* is why you have come. To take what is mine." Jaw clenched, he catapulted to his feet and kicked over the chair.

Irate men glowered at her on every side as she rose. "I offer you a partnership against Mateo, and the threat posed by my uncle and enemy werewolves. Asking only this in return."

Santiago's eyes were phosphorous slits. "You ask a great deal, Number Seven. If I concede to your demand and you do not honor your agreement, we will fall upon you and the Wapicoli like a scourge of scorpions."

Shaken more than he could ever know, she lifted her chin. "We will not fail you."

Pray God, she was not forced to choose between him and his kind, and Uncle Don.

She didn't waver. "While I'm sharing information, Lilith spells her brew. You might want to get your shine elsewhere."

He weighed her with a cross between cold fury and bemusement. "Who are you?"

"I've already said." She held out her hand. "The fang, if you please, and we have ourselves an accord."

With infinite reluctance written in every taut line, Santiago jerked the necklace from around his throat. Thrusting it into her palm, he growled. "We shall meet again Morgan Morcant. Your powers had better aid us."

"And yours us. The Wapicoli will rely on our new ally."

Head held high, she turned and walked away, her back burning from the fire in their eyes. Her knees threatened to give out and her insides were jelly, but she clutched the fang in her trembling hand.

She'd won the clan a much needed truce.

## Chapter Sixteen
## Warlock Among Them

Was that a reptilian scent mixed with the stink of sulfur from the fires of Mordor? *Yep*. Morgan was back at Lizard Hollow, the same damp chill in the air. The sunless afternoon didn't lend any cheer to the infamous clearing. Neither did the sinister mist hanging over the leafless branches and underbrush.

*Stay true to the quest*, she silently repeated, loathing the thought of meeting Lilith's half-lidded stare again.

Grim resolve kept Morgan hanging on. She had to see this through for Jimmy's sake. By heaven, if Lilith put one toe out of line, she swore she'd separate it from her webbed foot.

Jackson halted the assembly in the trees beyond the house, to scope out their surroundings before proceeding. "Here gathereth the Fellowship of the Fang. Thanks to our Lady Morgan who procured said fang for us," he said quietly, the prize tucked in his buckskin pouch.

"With blue light escaping the daggone cave," Ray marveled under his breath, tipping his camo cap at her. "Hats off to you, my lady."

"Freakin' awesome," Jimmy chimed in. "Like you had a magic wand, only you didn't. *Be the wand, baby*."

"My new motto." Scarcely able to believe her

success, and still a little weak from the energy it required, she smiled faintly. "You guys may not thank me when you have to meet the terms of my agreement with Santiago."

"As long as he upholds his end of the bargain, and no Mountain Panteras slice and dice us, we'll hail it a victory," Jackson assured her. "Ready for part two of our quest, gang?"

Rafe saluted him. "To infinity and beyond."

"And so say all of us," Hawthorne affirmed, from beside Dilly.

"Heartening to hear." His face muted, Jackson surveyed the vastly varied group. "But not everyone has to go inside with us. Morgan and I blocked Lilith before."

"With all-out, fight to the death effort, as I recall," she murmured.

He circled a strong arm around her. "We can battle the rays again. Some of you might want to wait by the trucks."

*Dang*, Morgan wished she could.

Ahead of them, beyond the hazy tangle of trees, bushes, frost-bitten weeds, and junked vehicles, were the outlines of the frame home, its chipped white paint and rusty roof. *Hell House*, as she'd come to think of it.

"Jackson's right. Not everyone need suffer," she agreed. "Some of you can hang back. Jimmy kind of has to go along."

"Lucky me." The kid consoled himself by biting into the last remaining cupcake.

"Nawww." Mato shook his head. "We gotta back you guys up. Any Wapicoli knows how to avoid her gaze. And I do." He glanced at Joe. "Not sure about you, old man. Don't need another space cadet on our hands, if you get zapped."

"Don't old man me," Joe muttered, hands thrust in his pockets, hunkered in a camo coat like Ray's. "We warlocks can take care of ourselves."

*If he really was one.* Morgan hated to offend him by demanding proof, but exposure to Lilith was highly risky.

"Please don't take any chances," Dilly pleaded. "Mama's always spelling my friends. Can't bring anybody home."

Joe's brow furrowed in his grizzled face. "Poor girl. That's not right. Someone needs to stop this witchy woman."

"Jimmy will tell you all about his scheme—*later,*" Jackson stressed. "We've got to get going. Is the coast clear?"

Multiple pairs of eyes peered through the haze at the potential war zone. As before, the blankets lining the porch rail signified the latest batch of shine ready for sale.

"Mama's there, or out at her still. I don't see anyone else." Dilly's voice was higher than normal. Returning to the hollow must've set every nerve on edge. "When we get a bit closer, I'll pop in and fetch a few of my things."

By *pop*, Morgan knew she meant literally, in a puff.

A truck backfiring cracked through the trees like they were under attack. Everyone ducked down behind the trunks. "That'll be Big Red. He runs shine for Mama," Dilly whispered.

"One of the giants?" Morgan would rather avoid

those.

A dip of her blue parka, and Dilly gestured for them to stay low. "With the temper of a bear. Sorry, Mato. Jethro might be riding along. He's no better than a low bellied snake. How about I head on toward the house? They won't think nothing of my coming. When they're gone, I'll signal you."

"Two less bad boys to tangle with works for me," Hawthorne said, to an undercurrent of agreement. "Are you sure you're up for this? Might run into your mom."

Her lower lip between her teeth. Dilly nodded. "She might cuss me out, but can't make me stay. If you fight Big Red and Jethro and the shine doesn't get run on time, she might not reverse Jimmy's spell for nothing. She's that spiteful."

"No point in going out of our way to annoy her." Jackson laid his hand on Dilly's shoulder. "We appreciate you running interference. Holler if you need help."

"That goes for me too, girl," Joe said gruffly.

"Thanks." She crept forward with the wariness of a deer, her blue parka and red hair a ray of color in the whiteness and general atmosphere of dilapidation.

*Heck*, throw in a haunted graveyard, it would fit. And some zombies. Wait—what was that?

The distant high-pitched wails of coyotes added to the overall creepiness factor, and stood the hair on the nape of Morgan's neck on end. Some people freaked at mice, she shivered at the unearthly yips and yowls from coyotes. Wolves had an innate dislike of these lesser canines, and vice versa.

She swallowed hard, her throat dry. "Sounds like a pack on the prowl. Are any of them shifters?"

Jackson tilted his head, listening. "They can be. Sneaky devils, too." A low male chorus supported his ruling.

"I got bit in the leg once. Whipped around and it was a coyote shifting into a man," Ray confided. "Not too smart. I snapped his scrawny neck," he added, with satisfaction. "Others of 'em are craftier, though."

"Much," Mato said emphatically, as if from firsthand experience.

"Great." Another potential source of attack. "Is anything or anyone in these mountains normal?"

Jackson considered her. "Define *normal*."

"I can flat out tell you, no, they're not," Ray said, to assenting nods. "A few hikers might be OK. Some tourists, couple of valley residents."

"But don't eat them," Rafe teased. "Against the rules."

"Tell me about it." Ray spoke again.

Letting the hushed debate pass, Joe ran his fingers over the reddish, gray-streaked hair beneath his cap. He was intent on what lay ahead. "I swear I know this place."

Ray angled his head at him. "Thought you'd never been here before?"

"Feels like a bad dream, but I'm thinking it wasn't."

"Uh huh," Jackson agreed. "We all feel that way about Lilith."

Morgan wholeheartedly concurred.

"I'll know when I see her." Joe rubbed a bristly chin.

Ray rounded on him. "You're not supposed to look at her."

Joe frowned. "I told you I can take care of myself."

A scowl creased Mato's noble face. "Man, you're pigheaded. Are we gonna have to blindfold you?"

"I need to be sure of something," Joe hissed. "The only way is to see the witch."

"Not in her dad-blamed eyes," Ray shot back. "What's so all fired important, you gotta risk getting yourself spelled?"

"I've gotten to wondering if Dilly—might—" Joe faltered.

"What?" Hawthorne startled like he'd been jolted with electricity. "You're way too old for her, man."

"Not that, nimno," Joe snapped. "It's just, well, she might be my daughter."

All eyes turned on him, and jaws dropped.

"You and Lilith?" Jackson's shock reflected Morgan's disbelief, and the revulsion turning her stomach.

Joe flushed and stroked his mustache with callused fingers. "It was a long time ago, but Dilly would be the right age. And I was drunk. Really, really drunk."

A shudder shook Hawthorne. "The only possible explanation."

"Or Lilith fried your brain like a hoppy toad," Ray suggested.

"Both possibly," Joe admitted, growing redder. He was gonna wear that mustache off with his nervous tugging. "There's something about Dilly I noted right off. We're kind of alike in that way," he continued.

Mato raised both hands, as if in an appeal to heaven. "What?"

Joe didn't stick around to answer the question. A familiar *poof*, and he was gone.

"Lordy," Morgan gulped, staring from her stunned companions to the male figure out in front of them in the haze closer to the house. There was no mistaking Joe.

"Whew." Ray gave a low whistle. "Well, I'll be. So he's a—what do you call it?"

"Teleporter," she supplied, between slack jaws.

Rafe pushed back his hat for a closer look at Joe appearing and disappearing in the mist. "He's popping around like a jumping bean. Explains how he gets by us quick and quiet like."

"How he's there and then not there." Mato gaped ahead. "But he never did it right in front of us."

"Wonder what else he can do?" Jackson spoke for them all.

Jimmy licked the last of the cupcake from his sticky fingers. "Put a force field around himself. I saw, during the party. It kind of warbled in the light."

"Warbled? You mean shimmered?" Jackson pressed.

"Maybe," Jimmy shrugged. "It was after Uncle Don came, so I didn't look for long."

Morgan had been too floored to notice. "No, you wouldn't. Not after that freaked out mess. I still can't get my head around it, or him."

"Forget normal. There is no normal," Jackson muttered. "Embrace weird."

Chapter Seventeen
Serpent Child

*Well, well.* Who should open Lilith's clawed and dented front door, but Dilly's older sister, Eve. Morgan immediately made that deduction and took an instant dislike to her.

The sisters were as dissimilar as sunbeams from the dark side of the moon. Eve's wintry blue eyes, white-blond hair, willowy figure, and cold beauty was a total contrast to the outgoing, curvaceous Dilly. While Joe had likely sired the warmhearted redhead, Lucifer must've spawned Eve. She struck Morgan as the sort who'd thrust a knife into your chest and turn it without blinking. The ice queen seemed friendly by comparison. Here, was evil personified.

Eve ran her chilly gaze over the assembly on the stoop. "Mama's been expecting you, Jackson." Her frosty eyes touched Morgan and Jimmy. "And you two." She gave a short laugh. "See you've got your entourage with you. Shifters, I suppose."

"Fellowship," Jackson corrected, grit in his tone, "and we also have a warlock." He nodded at Joe, who'd rejoined them. "If you'll please get your mother without delay."

"In a hurry, are you?" Eve scoffed.

"Yes." Gold glinted in his eyes. A warning, if Eve had any sense. Antipathy toward her was palpable in the group.

Morgan wanted to take her down, but checked herself for Jimmy's sake. Business first, then retaliation.

"Very well. If you don't want to play. Do make yourselves at home while I get Mama." Oozing sarcasm, Eve waved them in with a pale, meticulously manicured hand. She turned in her minus-zero size jeans and tiny blue halter top, skin like pearls.

Apart from being a card-carrying bitch, what powers did she possess? Morgan detected no hypnotic eye rays, or lizard scent. She smelled heavily, sickeningly, of gardenia, enough to overwhelm a funeral parlor. Morgan had the sneaking suspicion the floral tide was hiding something, while Dilly's use of perfume was simply because she liked the scent.

Besides, everyone except Dilly already knew she was a witch. Where the girl had gotten to, was anyone's guess. Probably popping in and out, squirreling away more of her stuff out by the clump of trees to truck back to the lodge.

The group followed Eve and, *Ugh.* Morgan found herself back inside the gaggingly smoke-filled room with traces of gardenia from Eve. Sight and scent of her set Morgan off, and she itched to get at her.

*Be the wand,* she repeated, liking Jimmy's spin, and holding herself in readiness should the occasion arise.

Eve didn't seem overly fond of her either and promptly left, lessening the oppressive sense of imminent destruction. Everything in the rundown room was the same as Morgan remembered, except—
"Lilith's got a disco ball?"

The glitzy multi-faceted globe, leftover from the 80s, hung like a spaceship from the stained ceiling. Morgan could say, 'Will wonders never cease,' only this wasn't wondrous, but just plain wrong. "Why on earth?"

"Mama always wanted one, and for a band to play in here," Dilly disclosed, and Morgan realized she'd rejoined them.

"Never in a million years," Ray bit out, "and don't any of you get yourself spelled into agreeing to it."

Joe grunted. "Scout's honor, and I was one."

Head tilted back, Hawthorne surveyed the glittering ball. "How many pieces do you reckon that thing would smash into?"

Blood drained from Dilly's face and her eyes were stark. "We're not gonna find out. Mama's dangerous enough as it is."

"You've got that right. Give it up, Hawthorne." The heat and smoke were taking a toll on Morgan, and she was already fading from dealing with Santiago. "Not sure I have enough strength left to oppose her wrath fully unleashed."

"Don't go looking for trouble," Jackson cautioned, grasping Morgan's hand. "Remember, we're stronger together."

She relished his touch and him. Even now, in this grim setting, he was so darn good looking he made her heart skip. "You may have to carry more than your fair share this time."

The pressure on her fingers tightened. "Done."

Joe came to life. "Might be something I can do to lift my weight in the fellowship. Sorry, Morgan, I'll have to leave you, Jackson, and Jimmy out of the circle, so you can complete the quest. But I'll protect the others." He motioned at her and Jackson. "If you'll step a little apart from the rest."

Uncertainty in his eyes, and similar doubt in Morgan, Jackson propelled her and Jimmy a few steps ahead of the pack. Could Joe actually carry this off?

Surrounding faces reflected Jackson's hesitancy as Joe raised his hands, circling them in slow revolutions. If Morgan hadn't watched, she'd have missed the transparent shield forming around everyone except them. Jimmy was right; the protective bubble did kind of warble.

Hands upraised, eyes slitted in concentration, Joe remained in place. "Not sure how long this'll hold."

"Long enough, I trust." Jackson turned toward the door. "Lizard alert. She's coming."

Did Joe realize Lilith was a demon lizard when he'd slept with her? Probably not. No one could be that drunk.

As before, she breezed into the room, as well as one of her bulk could breeze, in the fuzzy pink robe and polka dot boots. She halted abruptly, her broad face creasing, hooded eyes crinkling. Brushing back reddish strands escaping her pink hair tie she snuck furtive glances at Joe.

*Seriously? He made her nervous?*

Lilith laughed, but it sounded forced. "Eve said we had company. Not who exactly. Quite a party in here."

Jackson laid his hand on Jimmy's head. "Not a long-lived one. The sooner you undo your spell on him, the sooner we go."

"Fine by me, if you've got what I want." She seemed distracted by the warlock, and not the evil entity who'd slammed them with whirlwind force on their last visit.

"We have it." The silver-capped relic flashed in the light of the disco ball as Jackson drew the fang from his pouch. He gripped it, chain and all, in his palm. "You first."

Were Lilith's pudgy fingers actually fluttering? It appeared so as she cupped Jimmy's cheeks, with him giving her a look to kill the devil himself. She didn't comment on his simmering fury, unusual for her, but gazed into his blue glare. Morgan tensed, eye contact had enacted the spell before, but she supposed the same was necessary in order to reverse it. Jimmy regarded his nemesis like a caged tiger from behind his glasses.

"The spell is broken," Lilith intoned. "Repeat after me, I will not walk off a cliff on the next full moon."

Jimmy recited the revised version in a robotic tone, and she released him, snatching at Jackson. "Now gimme."

Loathing written on his face, he surrendered the toothy heirloom. "There had better be no more spells on the Wapicoli or our allies, which now include the Mountain Panteras, or you will receive a lovely parting gift. Or maybe, not so lovely."

Jimmy didn't hesitate. "I'm getting her anyway. I'll be back, witchy woman."

"Sure you will, kid." Grinning with some of her former mirth, probably because she had her prize, she waved them toward the door. "Go on, then. I've got business to tend to." She beckoned at Dilly. "Get on up to your room."

"Can't," she whispered, indicating the protective bubble Joe still kept in place. "Don't want to, anyway."

"Stupid girl. I'm surprised those werewolves haven't torn you in pieces. When that shield comes down, march up the stairs."

"It's not coming down from her," Joe growled. "Or did you think I'd forgotten our tryst, Lilith Dubois?"

Her face, the texture of ancient parchment, paled. "That was only one night, years ago. Didn't mean nothing."

"I'd agree, only, you've got something of mine," he countered.

"What?" Lilith squeezed out, as if an elephant had taken up residence on her expansive chest.

His bluish-gray eyes were scary dark. "My daughter."

A gasp escaped Dilly, who slumped against Hawthorne. He kept her from sliding to the floor.

"Sorry to tell you this way, girl," Joe apologized, "but I see you need my help." His blackish-brown gaze, like eyes that belonged to someone else, honed in on Lilith. "I don't know if you realized what I was that night, but I sure as hell didn't know about you. Dilly's coming with us. Whatever plans you had for her, stuff 'em. She has a father and friends now. You don't want to take us all on."

Lilith's chins quivered in outrage, but she was mute. They'd won this round.

Eve slunk into the room, her aura the kind of green associated with black magic. If possible, it was more insidious than Lilith's. "Let Dilly go, and good riddance. We won't miss her anyway. You've got me, Mama."

"When you're around," Lilith muttered.

Hands on her hips, Eve tossed her pale head.

"Which is plenty. I can't be here every second." She pointed a frosted pink fingernail at her younger sister. "Besides, I'm worth heaps more than Dilly when I am. What a moron."

"No argument there." Lilith waved Dilly off like a queen dismissing a tiresome subject. "Get on with you, then."

Dilly's tearful sniff and lip quiver tore at Morgan, and Eve's superior smile goaded her. "Hasn't that poor girl been beaten down enough?"

Whatever power Eve possessed, it was time for her to learn what she was up against. Her lizard mother already had a taste. Summoning her remaining energy, Morgan lifted her hands and flicked them at Eve. "Leave Dilly alone."

Blue light crackled from her fingers and the serpent sister reeled. Another zap, and Eve was on her knees. Whipping off her scarf, Morgan snapped it out around Eve's neck, and jerked her to the floor. Just as quickly, she whisked the length of wool back and restored it to her neck.

"*Now*, we'll go," she said, not missing the cold rage in those blue eyes. She'd made a new enemy.

## Chapter Eighteen
## The Hatchling

"You awake?" Jackson nudged Morgan gently, her head nestled against his shoulder where she'd slumped beside him on the couch. He smelled of the wind-blown forest, tangy wood smoke, and his own unique essence she found deeply appealing. Between his encompassing warmth and the woven blanket, she was more content than she'd been in days.

Stirring drowsily, she glanced around the main room of the lodge. Vibrant garlands of leaves accented with acorns and bittersweet berries still entwined the rafters, trailing down the log walls. Great orange pumpkins, the ones left uncarved, and colorful bunches of Indian corn tied with twine added to the fall flavor left from the party. The autumnal décor would probably last through Thanksgiving.

Assuming the Wapicoli celebrated the holiday associated with tribal genocide. She'd have to ask, but a more pertinent question occurred. "What time is it?"

"Five o'clock in the afternoon, or midnight. Take your pick. Doubt you'd know the difference," Jackson teased.

"Probably not." She yawned, vastly relieved to be back at the lodge, their mission accomplished.

"It's seven in the evening." He pressed his lips to her cheek. "You were mighty today, Wolf Girl."

"So were you." She'd been glad to let him handle the spell breaking session with Lilith.

Drained from drawing on her newly found powers, it was all Morgan could do to reach the truck afterwards. Zapping Eve had taken more out of her than she cared to admit, the drive back to the lodge a blur.

She rubbed her bleary eyes. "Did we eat yet?"

"Yeah. *We* did. Not you." He handed her a mug of hot milky tea, the inviting aroma making her realize how hungry she was.

Miriam bent near them with a plate of freshly made cornbread slathered in butter. "I've heard of your doings, Morgan, and am highly impressed, though not certain about you going after Eve."

Neither was Morgan, in hindsight, though she was glad she'd defended Dilly. Saying nothing, she gratefully accepted a chunk of cornbread and a napkin.

"I suppose your clash with her was inevitable, though," Miriam added, matter-of-factly.

"Eve had it coming," Jackson concurred. "I was tempted to do something myself."

"But you were more controlled," Morgan said between refreshing sips and buttery bites.

"Don't dwell on Eve. You're amazing, Morgan. I couldn't be prouder." The soft voice belonged to Aunt Maggie.

She tilted her head to discover the petite woman curled in a chair near the hearth, wrapped in a red and black wool blanket. "You saved our Jimmy." Tears glistened in Aunt M.'s blue eyes, the hue of twilight spangled with the first stars.

Relief mingled with the guilt stinging Morgan ever since she'd left Santiago's cave. "Yes, thank the Lord, but I threw Uncle Don under the bus."

"You didn't throw him, he dove. Actually, he was pushed. By me." Aunt M. blotted her eyes on a crumpled handkerchief.

Miriam clucked reprovingly. "You mustn't endlessly blame yourself. As for what you did, Morgan, rescuing Jimmy and gaining the clan an ally and one less pack of Panteras to battle is no small feat."

"Amen to that. No use in berating yourself, Maggie," Ray interjected from the corner. Morgan hadn't yet noticed his presence in the shadows dappled with firelight. "Many of us carry regrets too deep to fathom."

Given his *misdeeds*, putting it mildly, Ray would be a good one to commiserate with Aunt M.'s failings. But he wasn't alone. Jackson's father, Peter, lowered himself into a sturdy chair made of vines and bent twigs and sat near the shaken woman. He regarded her with an intensity Morgan had never observed in the man.

Considering Peter seldom opened his mouth, he did so now willingly enough. "You and Ray aren't the only ones who've chomped where you shouldn't. We all wrestle with the wolf. Sometimes we lose." He gestured at Aunt M.'s battered cheeks, unheard of sympathy in his dark gaze. "You've paid dearly."

"And will continue to, if Don has anything to say on the matter—" Her voice broke.

"He doesn't." Peter spoke with a protective air. "Remember, you're staying here with us. We'll see to it. I won't allow that madman near you."

This conversation definitely had Morgan's attention. Fast waking up, she gaped at Jackson. What the heck? Make that *holy heck*. "*WTHH*," she mouthed at him.

His expression resembled someone who'd landed among alien life forms. Brows arched, eyes wide, he shook his head.

"Well, if we're going down the regret road," Joe interjected, from a chair he'd taken, "I have one or two. Not that discovering I'm the father of such a wonderful girl isn't great and all. It's her mother—"

Ray held up a cautioning hand. "Say no more. Seriously."

No one wanted to go there. Fortunately, Hawthorne, Dilly, Rafe, and Jimmy were absent from the room. Mato had dropped off his passengers at the lodge and headed on in his pickup with the promise to return if needed. Ray, Rafe, and Joe were leaving tomorrow. Same deal.

'Thus endeth the Fellowship of the Fang,' she vaguely recalled Jackson saying, before she collapsed on the couch.

Miriam grew brisk as she handed round the corncakes. "No use in dwelling on past mistakes. All we can do is the best we're able with the time we have left."

Peter nodded his dark head, his hair worn back in a long braid over his plaid shirt. Ray and Joe solemnly did the same.

"Onward ho, and all that," Morgan managed, after another swallow.

Jackson raised his fist. "Full speed ahead and damn the torpedoes! Or something like that."

She couldn't think who he was quoting, but it made her smile. "That's the spirit."

Aunt M. carefully wiped her normally pretty face

with the hankie, wincing at the slightest pressure, and ran her fingers over tousled blond curls. In addition to her frantic flight through the tangled forest to reach the lodge, and the damage that did, Uncle Don must have struck her before she broke free. So totally unlike him, but the evidence was plain on her cheeks and jaw.

"Tell me the truth, Miriam, is there any hope for Don?" Aunt M. pleaded.

The wise healer regarded her for a long moment. "If he would agree to undergo the herbal treatment Morgan recently completed, then perhaps. I know of no other cure."

Sorrow clouded Aunt M's liquid gaze. "He'll never cooperate with us, unless we capture him and tie him down. Even then, I doubt it. I fear he's power crazed."

"Being a werewolf can go to your head." Empathy wafted from kind Miriam.

Morgan sensed the truth of her assertion. "It wasn't only the herbs you gave me that brought about my cure. Grandma Sarah also ministered to me."

No one pointed out that Sarah Daniel had been dead for two centuries. The unusual and weird were readily accepted in down-the-rabbit-hole land.

Aunt M. sniffed, and blotted her nose. "I'm sorry I wasn't able to be there for you."

"You're here now." Peter's voice was gruff with emotion.

A softer light filled Aunt M.'s gaze. "Yes. And I intend to do my fair share. I'm skilled in arts and crafts, and can make whatever you need me to."

Peter laid his hand on her shoulder, a caring in his manner that blew Morgan's mind. "Time enough to decide that when you're fully mended."

"*Megwich*, Peter," Aunt M. replied shakily, laying a hand over his in an unarguably intimate gesture.

*Holy freaking Moly*. Apparently, a lot happened between those two while the fellowship were off on their quest. Morgan battled the impulse to stare at them, openmouthed. Maybe she was still asleep.

"We did return, right? We're not under some spell, or in an alternate dimension?" Jackson whispered.

"Not sure. Jimmy would probably vote for the alternate reality thing," she whispered back. "Although, the place looks the same, smells the same…"

A world-rocking thought occurred, and Morgan arched her head to speak in Jackson's ear. They were seated a little apart from the others, and no one paid them much mind, but the room was full of werewolves with acute hearing. "OMG. What if they get married?"

"Before us?" He sucked in his breath like someone had punched him in the gut.

She gulped, as quietly as possible so as not to arouse suspicion. "You never said for sure we were getting married."

He shivered as if her whispery gasp had tickled his ear. "When have I had the chance? Plus, I'm not eighteen yet."

"Neither am I, for a year."

"Eleven months and 22 days. Not that anyone's counting." He closed an arm around her waist, sending exquisite ripples through her. "I'd marry you tonight, if Okema would allow."

"He won't. Good to know, though." Rapturous, wonderful, heavenly, sublime…she couldn't begin to express the emotion coursing through her.

"Yeah." The tenderness in his eyes said it all.

Jimmy chose that moment to tear into the room. "Egbert hatched!"

*Of course he did*, and no surprise in the name choice.

Jackson hailed the kid. "Let the feeding begin. We'll work it into the warrior training Okema wants us to focus on again. Now that Morgan's herself. Better even."

Jimmy sped back to the hatchling, via the kitchen.

Tomorrow, Morgan would return to perfecting archery, and mastering silent movement through the woods, throwing a knife in precise revolutions, scouting for enemy werewolves, now led by her uncle, and above all, preparing for the inevitable battle with Mateo. He'd come after her and Jimmy. He'd said as much. The derision in his black eyes flashed through her mind.

Evil was temporarily at bay, but war loomed over them like a lengthening shadow, and she was now one of the guardians of these ridges and Secret Valley.

Sudden realization struck her like an arrow. "I know what Eve is!"

Jackson's brow formed a question mark. "What?"

Miriam swiveled toward them. "A coyote."

"Yes. How did you know?" The woman never ceased to amaze Morgan, and he must be doubly wowed.

"The alpha female werewolf is always at odds with the alpha female coyote—*pashkwadjàsh*, in Shawnee."

"Of course." Jackson smacked his forehead, as though he'd missed the obvious.

Full comprehension dawned. So Morgan was now the alpha female among the Wapicoli? *Sweet*. And darn sobering. "Eve's also a witch. The bad sort."

"I figured." Miriam was a step ahead of her.

They'd gained the undivided attention of everyone in the room. Ray saluted her. "Brilliant deduction, Morgan."

A look of respect she never thought to see crossed Peter's expression. "Chalk up another formidable enemy."

Joe tipped his ever-present cap. "Let us know when you want to reconvene the fellowship."

"Will do." Jackson was pensive. "Good thing you've added to our allies."

Laying her empty mug aside, she considered. "What others do we have?"

He shrugged broad shoulders. "Bearwalkers side with the Wapicoli."

"Useful. Mato is great." She already missed his calm presence.

"Uh huh," Jackson grunted. "But bearwalkers are rare. Still waiting on the Star People."

They were rarer still. Skepticism nagged at her. "Do you really think they'll come back?"

"Only Okema knows. He hasn't advised us as to their ETA. Estimated time of arrival," Jackson explained.

"Ah." Even if Okema enlightened them, which he rarely did, he was pulling his Secret Warrior stuff.

"They'll come. You'll see," Miriam said, with near religious fervor.

"Right." She was a descendent, and consequently, Jackson. Still, it kind of felt like waiting on *The Great Pumpkin*. "Meanwhile, we have battles to ready for," Morgan said.

A smile hinted at Jackson's mouth. "And a thunderbird to train named Egbert."

*Whoa.* A vison of the monstrous creature dive-bombing their enemies, lethal talons outstretched, sailed through her mind. "Now *that* will make a terrific ally! Jimmy will be thrilled."

Jackson entwined his fingers with hers. "So will I. As long as we train him together."

"*Together.* I like the sound of that." Morgan nestled back against him with a happy sigh.

### A word from the author...

Married to my high school sweetheart, I live on a farm in the Shenandoah Valley of Virginia with my human family and furbabies. An avid gardener, my love of herbs and heirloom plants figures into my work. The rich history of Virginia, the Native Americans, and the people who journeyed here from far beyond her borders are at the heart of my inspiration. I'm especially drawn to colonial America and the American Revolution. In addition to YA fantasy romance, I also write historical, time travel, and paranormal romance, plus nonfiction.

www.bethtrissel.com

Thank you for purchasing
this publication of The Wild Rose Press, Inc.

If you enjoyed the story, we would appreciate your
letting others know by leaving a review.

For other wonderful stories,
please visit our on-line bookstore at
www.thewildrosepress.com.

For questions or more information
contact us at
info@thewildrosepress.com.

The Wild Rose Press, Inc.
www.thewildrosepress.com

Stay current with The Wild Rose Press, Inc.

Like us on Facebook

https://www.facebook.com/TheWildRosePress

And Follow us on Twitter
https://twitter.com/WildRosePress